THE
GIFT

BOB MOSELEY

A Novel

North Carolina

Published in the United States by BQB Publishing
(an imprint of Boutique of Quality Books Publishing, Inc.)
www.bqbpublishing.com

979-8-88633-000-7 (p)
979-8-88633-001-4 (e)

Library of Congress Control Number: 2022949531

Book design by Robin Krauss, www.bookformatters.com
Cover design by Rebecca Lown, www.rebeccalowndesigns.com
First editor: Caleb Guard
Second editor: Andrea Vande Vorde

PRAISE FOR THE GIFT
AND
AUTHOR BOB MOSELEY

"The Gift, like so many playing careers, is an exciting, emotional roller coaster. It's full of ups, downs, twists and turns, and over before you want it to be."

- Matt Merullo, former major league catcher with the Minnesota Twins and Chicago White Sox, and minor league manager

"Bob Moseley has crafted another memorable sports story that can be enjoyed by young and old alike. The story is more than another baseball hero story, it offers a tale about fleeting fame, redemption, forgiveness, and the enduring value of an act of kindness."

- T.M. Brown, author of the Shiloh Mystery series and president of Hometown Novel Writers Association

"A colorful journey through professional baseball that fans of the sport are sure to enjoy."

- Frank Wren, former general manager of the Baltimore Orioles and Atlanta Braves

CHAPTER 1

Tommy Browning slid onto a stool and lowered his head, staring at the vintage baseball cards laminated into the bar at Champs. His thick mop of hair tried to camouflage a dejected face.

"Hey, Tommy. How'd you guys make out tonight?" asked Pete, the bartender.

"We lost. I gave up six runs in the first inning," Tommy said.

Pete turned and poured a draft beer, plopping it down in front of the lanky pitcher for the Macon Peaches. He'd seen that pitiful face before, and he knew alcohol and a sympathetic ear was the prescription for that particular pain. Sometimes it worked, sometimes it didn't.

"Ouch, six runs? Sorry to hear that, but it will get better."

Tommy took a long swig and cast his eyes up at the barkeep. "I bet you Bob Gibson never did that in his lifetime." He glanced back down at the baseball card from 1967, encased for life in the Georgia sports bar.

"Probably not. That's why Gibson's in the Hall of Fame," Pete said, leaning forward. "One of the most dominant pitchers ever. Led the National League with a 1.12 ERA one season. I bet the Cardinals would love to have him again."

"Not as a corpse," Tommy fired back, revealing a slight smile.

"Well, I'll tell you one thing. If Gibson ever had a rough outing he always came back strong. You will too, Tommy."

Tommy's beer glass created an unsettling sound as he

lowered it onto the bar. "Pete, I'm playing my third season in Single-A. I gotta start pitching better or I'll get released. I should be in Double-A by now."

Pete recognized the sheer desperation in his voice. He'd heard it from many ballplayers before Tommy.

"Maybe I should make the call before they do," Tommy said. "Maybe I should get on with my life. I love baseball more than anything, but making $12,000 a year while chasing a childhood dream is kind of crazy. I can't live on that."

Tommy scratched the back of his neck, his fingers combing through an unruly head of hair. "With what I'm making, I have to substitute teach just to make ends meet. Funny how people think professional athletes all make good money. Not baseball players. Not unless you make The Show."

"Believe me," Pete said. "I've seen plenty of ballplayers pass through Macon. It's just a weigh station, Tommy."

"I mean, how long am I going to do this? I know it's only been a few years, but I'm trapped in Single-A, and major-league organizations don't have a lot of patience with twenty-second-round draft picks."

Pete slowly turned around. "See that guy up there." He pointed to an autographed Braves jersey hanging on the wall. "He was drafted in the twenty-second round. Turned out to be a pretty fair pitcher, a first-ballot Hall of Famer."

"John Smoltz," acknowledged Tommy. "Yeah, he was great, especially in the post-season." He took another swig of beer. "I probably should have played college ball and signed later. My parents wanted me to go to college, but I wanted to go pro. I got too swept up in the excitement when I was eighteen, a kid coming out of Newnan High. I always wanted to play for the Braves."

"How old are you now?"

"I'll be twenty-two in November."

"You're still young. You could develop like Smoltz . . . or Glavine . . . or Maddux."

Tommy offered Pete a crooked smile. "Right now I'm 0–5 with an ERA over six. I'm not fooling anybody at the plate."

"You really think they might release you?"

"Hell yes. And the minor leagues are shrinking all the time. It would be hard to hook up with another club. I might have to play in some independent league, and then you're as good as off the map."

"Hang in there, Tommy. Pitchers go through slumps just like hitters. It will get better."

"Maybe I just don't have the talent," he muttered, looking away. "I guess I should have known that from the start."

Pete turned and started up the popcorn machine behind the bar. He poured seed into a cup inside the popcorn chamber and, within minutes, popcorn began to fall. Tommy watched intently as the radical change from hard, ugly kernels to a fluffy white treat took place before his eyes. It was like the popcorn seed was able to reinvent itself through a wondrous transformation.

"Here," Pete said, sliding a wooden bowl full of popcorn in front of the dejected pitcher.

After listening to Tommy go on about his failed baseball career and watching him suck down three more beers, Pete felt that Tommy had cried on his shoulder enough. He was willing to dish out sympathy, but continuous whining crossed the line. Plus, Tommy was beginning to slur his words.

"Tommy, can I get an Uber for you? You should go home and get some sleep."

"Nah, I walked here and I can walk home," Tommy said.

He paid his tab and staggered out the door, wobbling down a dark street in the direction of his third-floor walk-up studio apartment. Humidity hung like a blanket in Macon—the kind of humidity that could make summer nights in Georgia a pitcher's toughest opponent. Shops were closed by now, but Tommy spotted an IHOP, so he went inside and plopped down in a booth.

"What can I get you tonight?" the waitress asked.

"Pancakes," he replied.

"What kind of pancakes would you like?"

"Flat ones," he blurted out, laughing at his own joke.

The waitress rolled her eyes. She was used to dealing with inebriated customers on the night shift.

She started to rattle off the variety of pancakes, but Tommy interrupted her with "buckwheat." Then he looked into his wallet. "Short stack," he added.

Tommy's red eyes focused on her nametag. *Wanda.* "Springsteen wrote a song about you," he said, "but I can't remember how it goes."

Wanda continued looking down at her order pad.

"I know, I'm originally from New Jersey," she finally said, lifting her head and humoring him with a forced smile.

"How long you been working here?" Tommy pried.

"About two months, darling," she said. "I'm trying to save up to buy a car."

"Me too," Tommy said. "I'm a player with the Peaches."

"Oh, we get a lot of you ballplayers in here," Wanda said. "You want anything to wash down those pancakes, maybe black coffee?"

"Just a big glass of water, please."

Within ten minutes, she returned with Tommy's order. "Thanks, Wanda," he said. "Hey, what time do you get off?"

Wanda had heard that question before. A somewhat

attractive blonde in her early thirties, she was used to handling the advances of young men desperate for late-night company.

"My shift ends at 6 a.m.," she said. "I don't think you want to stay up that long." She went to get Tommy his check. When she returned, Tommy was asleep, his head back and resting on the top of the booth with his mouth half-open.

"Wake up, darling. I brought you some coffee. It's on the house." She poured Tommy a cup, and he paid his bill, leaving a few dollars for a tip.

Stepping outside the IHOP, Tommy felt more awake thanks to the coffee. He looked at his cell phone. It read 11:25 p.m. Street lights were few and far between, but a full moon provided some visual relief. Tommy made a right on Magnolia Street. The city was dead quiet.

Suddenly, he heard a commotion down the block. The sound of punches, followed by screams and groans, emanated from a street corner, where a gang of teenagers was gathered.

Tommy ran over and caught a glimpse of the beatdown. "Stop!" he yelled, and the teens scattered into the night. A man was lying in the street, T-shirt ripped, blood oozing down his face.

"You okay?" Tommy stammered out as the man writhed in pain. He helped the man sit up on the curb, sensing that he was unable to stand. "What happened?"

"Just a second," the man responded, between heavy breaths. "Oh man, I think I broke some ribs."

"Just stay down for a minute. Rest up and tell me what happened."

"A bunch of punks jumped me. They beat and kicked me."

Tommy tried to get a better look at the man as he guided him toward a streetlight. He looked like he was in his late twenties or early thirties, although it was hard to tell with his coarse black hair and full beard.

"Can I take you home?"

"This *is* my home," the man shot back.

Tommy noticed a tattoo on the back of the stranger's neck. He zeroed in on the inscription: *Grace*. They sure didn't show him any of that, he thought.

Tommy waited another minute before announcing, "I'm going to lift you now. Try to get your feet underneath you." He placed his hands underneath the man's armpits and helped him struggle to his feet, despite the unnerving groans.

"I think I'd better get you to the hospital. Regency isn't far from here."

"No, no hospital. I don't have insurance."

"C'mon, you need to be checked out. Don't worry, they'll treat you even if you aren't insured."

The man reluctantly agreed. "You got a car?"

"No, we'll have to walk. I'll help you. It isn't far."

The man stumbled along with Tommy propping him up. "You've had an even worse night than me," he remarked.

"Why? What happened to you?" the man said, stopping for a few seconds to catch his breath.

"Oh, never mind. It doesn't matter." Tommy immediately regretted his flippant remark.

He checked in the battered man at the hospital's emergency desk and waited until the nurse brought him in to see a doctor twenty minutes later. "Hey, what's your name anyway?" asked Tommy.

"Eduardo," the man replied, not offering his last name.

"Okay, Eduardo, I'll wait here to see how you are."

Eduardo's eyes were filled with gratitude. But he said very little. He was too sore for conversation.

He was about to leave, but then he turned back and looked Tommy in the eyes. "Matthew 7," he said, managing an appreciative smile. "God bless you."

A bit bewildered, Tommy just nodded back.

About twenty minutes later the nurse returned to the waiting room. "I think he'll be okay, but we're going to keep him here tonight," she said. "He might have some cracked ribs. He's lucky you got there when you did. Did you file a police report?"

"No, they all got away before I could get a good look," Tommy said. "I guess they were taking it out on him because he's homeless. He was an easy target."

The nurse nodded. "Well, thanks for coming to his rescue. You may have just saved that man's life."

CHAPTER 2

That night Tommy lay awake in bed, thinking about his crumbling baseball career. He considered it amazing that he was playing professionally at all.

Back in high school, he never pitched regularly until his senior year. He was erratic on the mound, often losing the strike zone.

But midway through his senior year, the convergence of growth and fortune helped map out an unlikely future. A growth spurt pushed him up to an imposing height of six-foot-three, and his arm grew stronger. He started to throw strikes and found more bite on his curveball. All of a sudden he had considerable upside as a baseball player.

One day, an old man attended one of his Newnan High games. That man was known as a "bird dog," a part-time scout who works for an area scout. Bird dogs hope to spot a hidden gem, or someone with potential, and alert the area scout. They often beat the bushes at high-school games and summer leagues, mainly because they love watching baseball.

The bird dog invited Tommy to an open tryout in Rome, Georgia, telling him there would be scouts from the Braves in attendance. Hundreds of hopefuls sometimes showed up at open tryouts, but only a few were considered serious prospects. Tommy was allowed to pitch to three batters and struck out the side. He wasn't considered a prospect yet, but he was on their radar.

Then he pitched well in the state playoffs as a senior, grabbing a little more attention. In one game he struck out fourteen in a two-hit shutout. Tommy couldn't throw ninety miles per hour, but there was potential.

When the Braves drafted him, they sent him directly to Single-A instructional league. Even though he was starting at rock bottom, he couldn't wait for his first professional uniform.

After finally falling asleep in the wee hours, Tommy woke up late the following morning, staring at the ceiling from his old mattress lying on the floor. He called his nine-by-ten-foot room "the broom closet." Yet as cramped as it was, he preferred having his own place, rather than living with five other guys, like many of his teammates did. It was a place of his own, and he could take a girl back there if he ever got the opportunity. The room rented for only $300 a month.

He fumbled through his clothes that were scattered to the left of the mattress, and found his cell phone under his pants. No new calls or messages. He called Regency Hospital, but Eduardo had already been released.

Eduardo must have been okay, so he went back to worrying about his sagging baseball career. Time to take care of Number One again.

He tried to shake off the cobwebs from his evening at Champs and rode his bicycle to the ballpark early, even though he wasn't scheduled to pitch that night. He had to see Skeeter Jones, the Peaches' pitching coach. Skeeter was sitting in the dugout three hours before the game, going over some pitching charts. Tommy sat down next to him.

"Skeeter, did you notice anything wrong with my delivery last night? See any mechanical errors I can correct?"

Jones glanced up at Tommy and pulled off his black-framed reading glasses. He hesitated for a minute. Tommy squirmed during the silence.

"Tommy, Tom Seaver once said there are three components to pitching: velocity, location, and movement. Right now, you don't have any of the three."

He slapped Tommy on the back and erupted into a hearty laugh, but Tommy failed to see the humor in the situation.

"Now, Seaver used to say velocity might be the least important of the three, but we clocked you at eighty-four miles per hour on the radar gun last night. That ain't gonna get the job done, even in the minors."

Tommy lowered his head and looked away.

"I don't want to discourage you, son, but maybe you just don't have a major-league arm."

The pitcher was silent. He was watching his dream get stomped on right before his eyes.

"This is a tough business," Skeeter added. "Only about one out of every ten ballplayers drafted ever makes it to the big leagues."

"I knew that when I signed. But I know I can pitch better than last night."

"You know what? Billy the batboy might be able to pitch better than you did last night," Skeeter said, lowering his laugh to a chuckle this time. Tommy felt like getting up and leaving, but the coach quickly made an effort to comfort him, patting him softly on the knee.

"Y'all need to keep working at it. I can't help you today; I've got to go meet with Harrison, our starter tonight. But I can see you tomorrow and we'll go over some things in practice."

Tommy nodded. He just hoped he'd still be on the Macon

Peaches roster when Thursday arrived. Skeeter wasn't exactly reassuring. At a time when he desperately needed a confidence boost, he was being treated like a joke.

"Make sure you get your throwing in today," Skeeter called out as they parted ways. "Just light tossing."

Tommy waved back from shallow left field. He took that as a morsel of encouragement.

CHAPTER 3

In practice the next day, Skeeter grabbed Tommy in the bull-pen and ushered him to the mound, sidestepping the puddles from an early morning rain.

"Throw a few pitches for me," he suggested. "Bucky, come on over here and catch Tommy."

George "Bucky" Beavers hustled his stocky body over and squatted behind home plate. Skeeter watched silently with arms crossed as Tommy threw three fastballs and a pair of curveballs to the plate. "Curveball's not bad, but lawd we gotta do something about that heater," Skeeter commented.

For the next half hour, Skeeter adjusted Tommy's arm angle, release point, and the length of his stride, digging into his bag of pitching tricks designed to add up to ten miles per hour to a lazy fastball. They got mixed results. While the pitch may have gained a little speed, it was also harder for Tommy to control. Bucky blocked balls in the dirt and let several fly past him, nowhere near home plate.

Through the catcher's body language, Tommy could tell that Bucky was losing interest. He grew more and more lackadaisical in his efforts to glove the deliveries. That lack of enthusiasm infected Skeeter as well.

"Keep working on it," Skeeter said before departing for greener pastures.

"I gotta take batting practice soon," Bucky said, minutes after the pitching coach had left. "Maybe you can find another guy to catch you. If not, you can grab me after BP."

Tommy grabbed him by the shirt before he could leave. "Bucky, what do you think I should do? Any advice?"

"Try steroids." Bucky smiled playfully before departing.

There were no other catchers around, just pitchers. Tommy shrugged in frustration and went to shag fly balls in the outfield. The bullpen session seemed like a complete waste of time. It was even a step backward.

In his three-year professional baseball career, he'd never felt so low.

When practice ended, Tommy mounted his bike for the ride back to the "broom closet." He passed a statue in the square of Little Richard, the Macon native who was one of the architects of rock 'n roll, and he thought about getting something to eat at Subway but kept riding instead. After the late-night pancakes, he didn't even have money for a lousy sandwich.

However, an office with the words "Career Counseling" stenciled on the door brought him to a quick stop. *Why not check it out?*

He opened the door and found a middle-aged lady in office attire locking a file cabinet. "Can I help you?" she asked.

"Uh, yes ma'am. I just want to ask you a couple of questions if it's all right?"

The lady glanced up at the clock on the wall, which read 4:55 p.m. She placed her keys down on her desk.

"Sure, why don't you have a seat," she said with a smile. "My name's Janice Meadows. And you?"

"Tommy. Tommy Browning."

"Are you currently employed, Mr. Browning?"

"Right now I am, but that could change at any time," he replied, lowering his head. "I play for the Peaches."

"I see," she said with a slight chuckle. "You're not alone. I see ballplayers come into my office all the time. I know it can be a fragile career."

"Yeah, there's not a lot of job security."

"Well, I don't want to crush your dreams, but if you're looking for a new career, I might be able to steer you in the right direction. Do you have a high school or college diploma?"

"Just high school. I signed when I was eighteen and went straight to the minor leagues."

"Is that so," she said in a sympathetic voice. "Well, what could you see yourself doing outside of baseball?"

"I don't know. I've done some substitute teaching. Maybe I could teach full time."

"You could do that," Miss Meadows said. "But the state of Georgia requires a teaching certificate, which usually entails college credit hours. However, there are alternate routes to certification that attract candidates based on related experience. What would you like to teach?"

Tommy gave her a puzzled look. "I really don't know."

"How about going into coaching?"

"That could work," he replied. He was pleased to have at least one viable option.

Then came the damper. "Some schools prefer their coaches to also be Phys-Ed teachers at the school, but not all."

There was a moment of silence as Tommy weighed his options, before the counselor looked up at the clock and ushered the conversation to a close. "Why don't you contact the Georgia Department of Education to find out more about teaching or coaching?"

Tommy got up from his chair, thanked Miss Meadows for her time, and slid toward the door.

"Stop back in if you would like to talk some more and we

can make an appointment," she said. "In the meantime, I hope
your baseball career takes off."

CHAPTER 4

Friday night's game against the Greenville Goats was a disaster from the start. The Peaches were rotten, committing four errors over the first three innings. They even showcased a laughable Alphonse-and-Gaston blunder in the fifth when their second baseman and right fielder let a pop fly fall between them, each thinking the other would take it.

The Peaches trailed 9–0 in the sixth inning, and the hits—and walks—just kept coming. In the bottom of the eighth, Macon was down 15–3.

Tommy and a few of the other starters were out in the bullpen playing cards. They had the night off. Or so they thought. While some managers might have thrown in a position player to pitch at that point, Davey Concannon, a veteran of eight seasons in Macon, called Skeeter in the bullpen.

"Get Browning up. I want him to pitch the top of the ninth," Concannon said.

Skeeter broke up the card game. "Tommy, start warming up. You're gonna get the last three outs."

Tommy dropped his cards in disbelief. *Mop-up relief? For a starter?* He couldn't voice his displeasure, but the frown on his face betrayed his emotions. This was rock bottom, and he interpreted the assignment as his last chance with the Peaches. Tonight, he would be pitching to save his professional career.

"It's all right, man. I'll warm you up," offered one of the other starters, showing empathy for a fellow pitcher in pain.

But just like the other day when he worked with Skeeter, Tommy had little command on the mound. He worried too much about his arm angle and release point.

"Just a second, Tommy. I gotta put on a mask and chest protector," said his catcher, darting away to grab the equipment. When he returned he offered the simplest advice he could think of: "Be yourself. Just throw strikes."

Tommy was still getting loose when the eighth inning ended abruptly with a Peaches player hitting into a double play.

"You're in, Tommy," Skeeter said. "Remember what we worked on in practice the other day."

Skeeter's advice wasn't exactly reassuring. Tommy made a decision as he hustled to the mound at the beginning of the ninth: Ignore the pitching coach. If he was going to go down, it wasn't going to be by changing his motion in some crazy experiment.

There were less than fifty fans left in the stands at Luther Williams Field, and they rapidly scurried for the exits while Tommy took his eight allotted warm-up pitches. Cheers wouldn't be his motivation. Fear of failure would be.

Bucky Beavers put down one finger for a fastball. Tommy gave him a quick nod. He wanted to throw a strike to start and not fall behind in the count with a breaking pitch. The Greenville batter immediately jumped on it and lined a sizzling single to left field.

From behind the plate, Bucky made a downward motion with his glove and free hand, telling Tommy to get the ball down. His first fastball didn't have much on it, and it was belt-high.

When the second Greenville hitter doubled into the alley, putting runners on second and third, a feeling of dread grabbed

Tommy by the throat. He caught a glimpse of Concannon dipping his head in the dugout.

"Let's get an out," the manager yelled out.

Tommy was both rattled and frustrated. Little mattered anymore. On his next pitch, he hastily grabbed the ball and heaved it, barely looking at the catcher's sign.

In that desperate moment, magic flowed from the arm of a struggling Single-A right-hander.

The ball came out of Tommy's hand slowly, dancing through the air like a butterfly, before suddenly picking up speed, crossing home plate, and landing with a thud in Bucky's glove. The Greenville hitter bailed out of the batter's box, and Bucky dropped his glove like he was handling hot coals. Even the home-plate umpire jumped back a foot before finally signaling strike one.

"Time!" Bucky jogged out to the pitching mound, still shaking his glove hand. "What in the name of God was that?"

"Uh, I don't know . . . I don't know where it came from," Tommy said, wide-eyed.

"Did you throw your two-seam fastball?" Bucky wondered.

"I don't know. I just kind of grabbed the ball and threw it."

"Try to do it again. I'll be ready for it this time." Bucky hustled back to his squatting position behind the plate, stopping briefly to give Tommy another dumbfounded look.

The catcher's sign was just for show. Tommy wound up and let the baseball fly again. He didn't throw the ball so much as it just seemed to spring from his hand.

"Strike two!" The pitch came in the same way, fluttering softly before taking off like a rocket. The poor Greenville batter was frozen again, so mystified by the movement of the ball that he couldn't even swing. Tommy threw it a third time with the same result: three pitches—all strikes. The hitter never even took the bat off his shoulders.

The beleaguered Greenville player looked blankly at the home-plate umpire, as if he wanted the ump to explain what he'd just witnessed, before shuffling back to the dugout. He stopped and told the on-deck hitter, "You're not going to believe the pitch this guy has. Good luck!"

That second batter managed a swing, but by then the ball was already in Bucky's mitt. He was retired on three pitches too.

Tommy's two dazzling strikeouts had a strange effect on him. They energized him and took his breath away at the same time. What was going on? Had he stumbled upon a new grip?

A few die-hard fans—the ones who remained and weren't gathering their kids for the drive home—rushed down to open seats behind home plate. They couldn't believe their eyes. However, manager Concannon was paying little attention to a 15–3 game. He was working on his lineup card for the next night.

Tommy mixed in his curveball to the third batter and missed the plate a couple of times, but he wound up striking out the side. He pumped his fist as he ran back to the dugout, a childlike spring in his step.

Skeeter greeted him warmly along with a handful of teammates. "Great job, Tommy! That bullpen session really paid off fer ya. Some pitchers surprise themselves after working with me."

Tommy just smiled. He was searching for an explanation too.

CHAPTER 5

A day after mopping up the Greenville Goats with an astonishing relief performance, Tommy stood in the Macon clubhouse at Luther Williams Field with pen in hand. He was about to offer his name on the list for "Player Appearances" conducted by the Peaches organization. The appearances were usually meet and greets with Peachy the mascot at civic events, car dealerships, or schools. They were designed to promote the ball club in Macon and surrounding communities.

The gigs usually paid $75 or $100, so they were coveted by the ballplayers. But even signing up early didn't guarantee you would be selected.

Manager Concannon happened by. "Tommy, you were awesome last night. You were throwing gas. We're going to start you in the opener in Asheville."

Tommy grinned from ear to ear. He *had* made an impression in the wee hours of the night. As good as it felt, he worried that the strikeouts might be dismissed as success achieved against a bunch of late-inning benchwarmers.

"Great, Skip. I'll be ready."

"You'll be rooming with Bucky on the road. The two of you can go over the scouting reports together."

The upcoming road trip consisted of two games in Asheville and a pair in Greenville before heading home down I-85 through Atlanta. Unlike some of the guys, Tommy loved road trips. They freed him from his claustrophobic apartment for a few days and you also got $30 per day in meal money. That meant something to a starving ballplayer. Plus, a pregame spread was provided, even though it was usually just sandwiches, pasta, and some fruit. You had to get there early because it was gobbled up fast.

Road trips often meant long bus rides, and the opening series was usually the longest. After traveling four hours and thirty minutes from Macon to Asheville, the Peaches were scheduled to check in to their hotel room and then go immediately to the ballpark for their game against the Tourists.

Far from optimum conditions for a starting pitcher to be at his best.

———

Late the next morning, Bucky threw his bags in the overhead compartment of the team bus. "No more room below," he said to Tommy, who was already seated with his bags stored. "You want the window or the aisle?"

"I'll take the aisle for my legs, if you don't mind," Tommy said, hoping to stretch out his long frame.

"You got it. You're pitching. I squat all game." Bucky bumped his head slightly on the overhead compartment as he maneuvered around Tommy to the window seat.

The two players reviewed the scouting report as the bus barreled north on I-75 toward Atlanta.

"Asheville is a good hitting team, but I know their hitters and I'm sure you do too. We play them so much," Bucky said. "I hope you have the same stuff you had the other night. That was incredible."

Tommy gave his catcher a nervous smile. "I guess I won't know until I warm up."

The conversation hit pause while Tommy contemplated the future. "Bucky, what is this, your third year in A-Ball?"

"Yeah, just like you. But this is my second organization. I signed with the Rangers first but got released after a year."

"Did you sign out of high school like me?"

"Nah. I'm from Texas, and I played two years at San Jacinto Junior College before signing. The Rangers released me when they drafted some hotshot high-school catcher in the fifth round and wanted to start him in Single-A."

"That sucks," said Tommy.

"You know, I don't know what that kid's doing now, but I thought I was better than him. Teams always favor players they're more invested in. It's just a hard fact." Bucky shook his head and grimaced. "In baseball, it's always easier to move up as a high draft pick. They want a return on their investment."

"Hey, tell me about it. I went in the twenty-second round and I'm stagnating in A-Ball."

"The other thing is, managers don't move up in the organization if they don't win, or if they don't develop the players that the big-league team wants. To make those guys better, they have to play them."

"Sometimes I think there's just a lot of luck involved in whether you make the bigs," Tommy said. "Being in the right place at the right time."

"And avoiding injuries," Bucky added.

"I'd give anything to play just one game in the major leagues," Tommy said. He wistfully gazed out the window as the bus passed the city of Atlanta and the golden dome of the state capitol. "Bucky, you ever think about quitting baseball? How many years are you giving yourself to make The Show?"

"I don't know. I originally said five years, but it's hard to get baseball out of my blood. I'll probably chase the dream for as long as I can, just like you. There's a lot of pressure though,"

Bucky conceded, after another moment of reflection. "I feel it every at bat."

"Try to relax. You're hitting close to .300 and you've got a lot of homers. Big-league teams are always looking for power."

Bucky quickly corrected Tommy. "I'm hitting .320. You'd think somebody would notice that and promote me."

"You ever ask Davey about that?"

Bucky laughed that off. "It's not like you can go to your boss and ask for a promotion. Baseball's not like working at Apple or Amazon. The front office tells you when you move up."

"I hear you, brother. Baseball is a business, but it controls you."

"Yeah, and Hal Bagley is an all-star. They're not looking for another catcher with the Braves right now."

"Well, you have to be on their radar. At least you're not a winless pitcher like me."

Bucky elbowed Tommy gently in his side. "Maybe your luck will change tonight. I have a good feeling about it."

Most of the players were nodding off with their headphones on as the bus followed I-26 West, closing in on its destination. When the bus pulled into the Econo Lodge, the late-afternoon sun was still high and the day was far from over.

"Just drop your bags in your room. I want you back on the bus in ten minutes," Concannon announced.

Tommy picked up his room key and tossed his bags on one of the twin beds, delighting in the thought of a firm mattress and a good night's sleep. But that all depended on his evening on the mound.

CHAPTER 6

A clear, starlit night in North Carolina drew a good crowd, and for the fans who attended the game, it was well worth the modest price of admission.

By the end of the second inning Tommy had six strikeouts; by the end of the third, Asheville still didn't have a baserunner; and by the fourth inning they were checking the pitcher's glove for foreign substances.

"He's got to be using something," yelled out the Tourists manager, Bud Giles. "A baseball doesn't move that way."

Giles kept riding the home plate umpire until the ump went out to check the glove. Nothing. Then the ump inspected Tommy's hands and uniform for a gel, emery board, or hidden instrument used to scuff up the ball and make it fly like a UFO.

Still nothing. The ump jogged back to home plate, shaking his head at Giles. "He's clean."

"He can't be. He's got the ball performing tricks," said an incredulous Giles.

The ump shrugged. "Play ball!"

Words of encouragement and backslaps greeted Tommy in the Macon dugout after every inning, but things changed heading to the seventh. His teammates grew distant, avoiding him in deference to baseball superstition. Tommy's pitching line through six innings: no runs, no hits, no walks, and sixteen remarkable strikeouts.

"His stuff's filthy. It ain't even fair," said one hapless hitter.

Tommy's own fielders struggled to maintain their concentration. So few balls were even put into play that it was easy to get mesmerized by the surreal summer evening. But no one wanted to get caught flat-footed with a perfect game on the line.

Offensively, the Peaches broke through with a solo homer by Bucky Beavers in the fourth and added an insurance run in the sixth. Asheville's pitcher was sharp, but not overpowering like Tommy Browning. The Tourists' lefthander had "hard-luck loser" written all over him by the seventh inning.

Tommy finally issued a walk in the seventh after mixing in a few curveballs that ran just off the plate. The perfect game was gone, but not the no-hitter.

"Just finish with your fastball . . . or whatever you call that pitch," Bucky advised. "Make them beat you with your best."

Tommy nodded and exclusively threw his mystery pitch the rest of the way. It was untouchable. Not only did the baseball dance out of his hand, it seemed to explode across the plate faster over the last two innings.

Two innings ago, Bucky had abandoned the senseless formality of flashing signs to his pitcher. He knew what was coming. All he had to do was catch it.

The lively Asheville crowd reveled in the performance, even if their beloved Tourists were the foils. The fans were nearly all on their feet entering the bottom of the ninth, clapping for their opponent.

When the first hitter showed bunt, there was booing from the crowd. He took a stab, but went down on three pitches.

The next Asheville batter made contact, but his late swing produced nothing more than a weak Little-League pop-up to first base.

Tommy was filled with the confidence of a superstar as he focused on his catcher's glove. Only one more out for his first no-hitter—on any level. He felt like he was dreaming.

His first pitch blew across the inside corner, making the right-handed hitter jump back. The batter took a good hack at the next one but came up empty. An 0–2 count, but no time to nibble. Tommy rocked back on the pitching rubber and fired away again.

Another laser beam delivery pounded into Bucky's glove with airborne artistry. The home-plate umpire pumped his fist emphatically to cap the minor league masterpiece: No hits, one walk, and twenty-two strikeouts. Macon 2, Asheville 0.

Tommy was mobbed as he jumped off the mound. He instinctively shielded his right arm from the celebration.

The party continued in Tommy and Bucky's room once the team bus arrived back at the Econo Lodge. Players and coaches wedged their way in, including Skeeter and Concannon, many bringing six-packs of beer with them.

Bucky welcomed the crowd with an ice pack on his swollen catching hand.

"Tommy do that to ya?" asked Skeeter, snapping open a can of Pabst Blue Ribbon.

"The price I pay for catching him. My glove needs more padding."

"Hey Skip, I wanna stay in this room next time," shortstop Frankie Torres said to the Macon manager. "Must be magical. These guys had some night!"

"Now you've got to top that. We want twenty-five strikeouts next time," outfielder Brian Blake said. Tommy was still in shock that he'd struck out twenty-two.

Several pitchers huddled around Tommy, begging him to teach them his secret pitch. "If I tell you, I'll have to kill you," Tommy replied with a sly grin. "This is classified stuff."

They all looked disappointed.

After an hour or so, Skeeter Jones and Davey Concannon

began to head to their rooms, warning the players not to stay up too late, like they were their children. Skeeter, who by that time had drained several beers and was feeling no pain, told Tommy he wouldn't use him for the rest of the road trip.

"Rest your arm. I'm gonna save ya for Greenville Tuesday at home. It'll help boost attendance."

"Great, but we have Hickory next week," Tommy gently reminded him.

"Daggumit, Hickory. That's what I meant."

Before they left, Concannon raised a beer in toast.

"Here's to Tommy Browning. If he can suddenly turn into Nolan Ryan, there's hope for the rest of you guys too."

When the players had all vacated the hotel room, around midnight, Tommy picked up his phone and called his parents, Evelyn and Harold, in Newnan.

His mom picked up her phone after six rings. "Tommy, are you all right? Why are you calling us so late?" she asked in a groggy voice.

"Mom, I pitched a no-hitter tonight!"

"Harold, come to the phone," Evelyn said, motioning her husband out of bed with her free hand. "Tommy pitched a no-hitter!"

Harold moved to the other side of the bed and grabbed the phone from his wife. "Son that's amazing. You told us the other day that you thought the Braves were going to release you. Now you pitch a no-hitter?"

"With twenty-two strikeouts, Dad."

"Twenty-two? Wow, I guess you showed the Braves a thing or two."

"Yeah, I've found a new pitch, and it's filthy," Tommy said.

Evelyn took another turn with the phone. "Be sure to thank your pitching coach."

"Mom, to tell you the truth, I don't think Skeeter had anything to do with it. And he was laughing at my struggles before last night."

Tommy paused for a second before adding, "Maybe my arm's just getting stronger."

"It probably is," Harold said. "You're still young and growing."

"Okay, I'm sorry to wake you up. I just couldn't wait to break the good news to you guys. Go back to sleep now."

"Thanks for calling," his parents chimed in. "Congratulations!"

"I'll talk to you some more tomorrow," Tommy said.

He hung up the phone, wondering if his arm actually *had* gotten stronger. It seemed as logical an explanation as any for his recent success.

CHAPTER 7

The next night, the Peaches lost in the bottom of the ninth but they took two games in Greenville and felt satisfied heading back to Georgia following a 3–1 road trip. But then the team bus blew a tire Sunday night on I-85, and the 223 miles back to Macon took six hours instead of four. The bus didn't pull into Luther Williams Field until 4:00 a.m.

The next morning, Concannon was dozing in his office when Ziggy Dale, public relations/promotions director for the Peaches, burst through the door.

"Don't you knock? I'm trying to catch some z's," said the manager, slowly straightening up in his reclining chair. He ran a hand over his morning stubble.

"Sorry. I heard you got in late."

"I slept here last night. Just get me some coffee."

Dale returned a few minutes later and handed Concannon a cup of joe. "You take it black, right?"

Concannon slowly lifted the coffee cup to his mouth and examined it through half-shut eyes before taking a sip.

"Ahh. All right, what do you want, Ziggy?"

I've got an idea for a promotion involving Tommy Browning. A no-hitter with twenty-two strikeouts—we've got a phenom to market."

Concannon put down his coffee cup and shook his head. "I hope this isn't another one of your crackpot ideas, Ziggy."

"What do you mean 'crackpot'?"

"Remember the contest for fans to see who could eat the

most peaches, gluttony gone wild? Half the contestants got sick and threw up."

"It would have worked out, but I think those peaches were a bit overripe," Ziggy conceded.

"And what about the parachuter who was supposed to land on home plate at the Fourth of July game? He overshot and flew into our dugout holding the American flag. I thought somebody was going to get impaled."

"A sudden gust of wind threw him off course. I had no control over that."

"It caused a panic. I still remember Skeeter and Whopper running smack into each other trying to get out of the dugout. They both fell flat on their backs. Must have been the first time in baseball history a team put a designated hitter *and* a pitching coach on the Injured List together."

Ziggy shrugged. "They both bounced back."

"All right, what about the contest for some lucky girl to win a date with Chad Boswell?"

"Over a hundred fans entered," Ziggy recalled. "Chad was a stud."

"Yeah . . . they did," Concannon said slowly. "But the winner was a gay guy! Our evangelical fans put up a stink."

Ziggy cracked a smile. "To his credit, Chad was a good sport and honored the date. They went out for dinner at Applebee's, as I recall, and had a good time."

Ziggy leaned forward in his chair. "Funny you should mention that last one. I was thinking we could run the same contest for a date with Tommy."

"You want to try it again?"

"Sure, and this time we'll lower the age a bit too, so girls eighteen and up are eligible." Ziggy's enthusiasm rose with his voice. "Tommy's a hot commodity. We'll give him $100 for the date. He'll be thrilled for a free night on the town."

Concannon wasn't inclined to discuss the idea anymore. "Sure, sure, try it again if you want," he said.

"I've also been thinking about a Tommy Browning bobblehead giveaway night. That could be a big hit."

"Yeah, yeah," Concannon said, waving his hands at Ziggy dismissively. "Get out of here now. I need more sleep."

Ziggy headed for the door, but suddenly stopped and looked back at the Macon manager. "Oh, one more thing. I'm going to refer to Tommy as the 'Browning Rifle' in press releases. We'll see if it sticks."

CHAPTER 8

By the sixth inning Tuesday night, a silent sense of anticipation bubbled through the crowd at Luther Williams Field. The newly christened Browning Rifle still had not misfired.

That made it fourteen straight innings of no-hit ball over his last two starts. Tommy Browning seemed unhittable.

Unhittable, but not unscored upon. In a fluke fourth inning, the Hickory Crawdads bunched a walk, a wild pitch, and a two-base throwing error into a 1–0 lead. Fluke, it seemed, because every out recorded was a strikeout.

The fact that the Peaches were losing made the possibility of a second straight Browning no-hitter more bizarre. Would the accomplishment be as great if the Peaches lost? Would the celebration be muted?

Bucky Beavers wasn't worried. "Just keep throwing them darts," he said to his pitcher, before taking his position behind home plate to open the sixth. "We'll get you some runs."

Frankie Torres squirmed and smoothed out the infield dirt with his feet. The shortstop felt responsible since his overthrow of first base allowed the Hickory run. He pounded his glove and focused as best he could. But Torres could be excused for struggling with his concentration. The grounder hit to him in the fourth inning was Hickory's only ball put into play to that point.

"Forget about that, man," said second baseman Henry Offerman, sensing his teammate's unease. He tossed Frankie the infield warm-up ball.

Just then an announcement came over the public-address (PA) system. "We have a winner in the contest to Win a Dream Date With Tommy Browning."

A hush fell over the crowd in eager anticipation.

"The lucky fan is Ellie Wainwright of Macon. Congratulations, Ellie!"

Polite applause—mixed with some wistful moans—flowed from the crowd, followed by a joyous scream, "Woo-hoo!"

Tommy remained focused and didn't even hear the announcement. He proceeded to sail through the sixth like he was on a Caribbean cruise, fanning the side again to run his strikeout total to eighteen.

"All right, let's get the guy a run," Concannon called out in the Macon dugout as the players stepped back in for the bottom of the sixth. He turned to Skeeter. "Do you believe this?"

The run finally came when Torres atoned for his throwing error by smacking a double down the third-base line, driving in Offerman. Beavers, wielding a hot bat, followed with a two-run homer for a 3–1 Macon lead.

"They look demoralized," Concannon said about the Crawdads. "They're not even making contact. How are they going to get any more runs?"

If a white flag were handy, Hickory would have waved it. The Crawdads did manage to put a bunt in play and a soft pop-up to third, but no ball left the infield. For the second game in a row, Tommy finished with twenty-two strikeouts and a no-hitter.

When the final out was recorded, Tommy jumped into his catcher's arms. The half-full stadium, made up primarily of die-hard Peaches fans who knew all about his dominance in Asheville, rose for a five-minute standing ovation.

Fans spilled onto the field for Tommy's autograph. Others

took pictures with their cell phones, capturing the moment for posterity. This was unquestionably the greatest moment in Macon Peaches history.

In the dugout, Davey Concannon gave Skeeter Jones a blank stare, his jaw dropped and his mouth agape. "Is this the same guy who couldn't get an out for us a few weeks ago?" he asked in disbelief.

CHAPTER 9

Nearly lost in the hysteria of back-to-back no-hitters was the fact that Tommy had a date to fulfill the next night.

Ziggy Dale reminded him. "The contest winner's name is Ellie Wainwright. She's nineteen years old and a big Peaches fan. She lives here in town, so you won't have to go far to pick her up."

"I don't own a car."

"You can use mine. I want this promotion to go well," Ziggy said. "Just make sure you have it back at the ballpark the next morning and drive safely. You're responsible for that young lady's welfare. Oh, and by the way, I recently dropped my collision insurance. Here's a hundred bucks." He pulled out a roll of five twenty-dollar bills from his pocket. "Show her a good time."

Tommy looked forward to the female companionship on his day off, and when he arrived at his date's apartment, he liked what he saw at the front door. Ellie Wainwright was a cute brunette with hair to her shoulders, big brown eyes, and a smile that could light up the night. She was pleasantly plump, and Tommy preferred his women that way. There was more to hug. Plus, she was dressed attractively.

Hi, Miss Ellie," he said with Southern politeness. "I'm Tommy Browning."

She gave him a warm hug. "*So* nice to meet you, Tommy. This is awesome. Who ever thought I'd be going out with the

superstar of the Macon Peaches?" She released her five-second
grip on Tommy, who wouldn't have minded if the hug lasted
even longer. "Where are you taking me tonight?"

"I thought I'd take you to Henry's on Peachtree Street in
Atlanta. The food is good, from what I hear."

"Cool! I'll get my things."

When Ellie returned, Tommy opened the passenger door of
Ziggy's Toyota Camry for her. She smiled in appreciation of his
manners before blurting out, "Congratulations on your second
no-hitter. You are amazing!" She cupped her hand on the right
side of his face. "Oh, you're starting to blush," she said with a
giggle.

To Tommy's surprise, Ellie actually wanted to talk baseball
on the ride to Atlanta. She was more knowledgeable than any
fan he'd ever met. She rattled off the name of every Peaches
player who ever made it to the big leagues. She could also talk
game strategy, noting that she was an all-conference softball
player in high school.

"What was Concannon doing the other night, letting Roberts
swing away with the winning run on second and no outs? I'd
have bunted him over so he could score on a sacrifice fly."

"Roberts is a terrible bunter," Tommy countered.

"Then tell him to hit behind the runner. He's a right-handed
hitter; he should be able to do that."

Tommy was impressed. "You should be managing the
Peaches, Ellie."

"If I were, I'd promote you," she said with a warm smile.

When they arrived at Henry's, Ellie was impressed. "You
know, I originally was thinking about wearing my Macon
Peaches T-shirt on the date. I'm glad I didn't. I didn't know
we'd be going to such a nice restaurant."

"You look great in what you're wearing," Tommy said. He

eased his eyes over Ellie's outfit: white slacks and a colorful summer top with a plunging neckline.

Dinner kicked off with Tommy ordering a Georgia Mule for each of them, a potent mix of bourbon, ginger beer, peach nectar, and fresh mint served in a copper cup.

Ellie looked at him cautiously. The waitress hadn't bothered to card her.

"You know I'm breaking the law," she said. "The drinking age is twenty-one."

Tommy smiled at her. "Don't worry. I'm driving."

Their entrées were also of Southern style, with Tommy ordering the fried chicken and Ellie shrimp and grits. Baseball still dominated the conversation, but Tommy began inserting questions to learn more about his date.

"I was born and raised in Macon," Ellie said. "They call it 'the Heart of Georgia.'"

"Do you work?"

"Do you? I don't consider baseball work," she joked.

Tommy shrugged. "I'm busy chasing my dream."

"I guess I am too," Ellie said. "I go to Georgia State. I'm trying to become a teacher."

"No kidding. I've done substitute teaching myself. I enjoy working with kids."

"That's my dream, teaching high school. It always has been," she said.

"What year are you in at Georgia State?"

Ellie barely got out the word "junior" when a visitor interrupted.

"Aren't you Tommy Browning of the Macon Peaches?" inquired the young boy, approaching their table and busting in on the conversation.

Tommy looked slightly annoyed at the abrupt intrusion but

thrilled at the same time that he was recognized. He soon broke into an appreciative smile. "One and the same."

"I don't believe it. I just saw your picture online. You pitched two no-hitters."

Tommy nodded.

"Can I get your autograph?" The boy, probably about twelve, dropped a pen and piece of paper on the table, and Tommy willingly obliged.

"Thanks, Browning Rifle." The boy scurried back to his table, where his parents both waved to Tommy, pleased that their son's request was honored.

"Wow. Do you get that much?" asked Ellie, leaning back and raising her shoulders to indicate she was impressed.

"That's probably the first time I've ever signed an autograph," Tommy said with a grin.

"Well, you may have to get used to it, the way you're pitching."

They shared a dessert of vanilla ice cream and butterscotch sauce over a blond brownie before paying the $85 tab and heading back to Ziggy's vehicle.

"I've got an idea," Tommy said as he reached into his pocket for the keys. "Do you want to get a bottle of wine and catch the sunset at Lake Oconee?"

Ellie's brown eyes got even bigger. "Sure, that would be fun."

They arrived at Lake Oconee by 8:30 p.m.—plenty of time to see a summer sunset—with a bottle of Merlot and two plastic glasses. A grassy knoll allowed a perfect view of the orange sun sinking over the tranquil lake.

"Let's go over there, away from the Sweetgum tree," Tommy said. "I hate those spikey balls they drop. They remind me of the coronavirus."

Suddenly, a white-tailed deer burst out of the woods, about fifty feet away. Tommy dropped into a crouch, like he was firing an imaginary shotgun aimed at the deer. "Pow," he said, for effect.

Ellie immediately shoved him to the ground.

"What did you do that for? I'm just playing around."

"How could you shoot that beautiful creature? Don't you like animals?"

"Uh . . . sure, I do," Tommy said.

"Oh yeah? What's your favorite animal at the Atlanta Zoo?"

The question came out of left field. Tommy thought long and hard before answering. He knew he had to come up with something good.

"The giraffes," he replied.

"Why, because they have long necks and are tall like you?"

"I like how they can see beyond where they are," he said. "They can see what's ahead in life—all the obstacles."

Ellie seemed impressed by his answer. "I like the lions, the lioness in particular," she said. "They're loving mothers, yet they're strong. They don't take any crap."

They sat down in the grass and opened the screw-top wine.

"Across the lake is the Ritz-Carlton," Tommy pointed out. "I'll take you there someday when I make The Show."

Ellie gave Tommy a big smile. She took that as an unexpected sign of commitment, although he may have been just trying to be funny.

"The Ritz-Carlton? That's awfully expensive," she said.

"When I'm in The Show, I'll have lots of money," Tommy said. A few weeks ago, he would never have made such an audacious boast.

After a glass or two, Ellie slipped in the question that every other pitcher was dying to ask. "So, I haven't asked you yet, how *do* you throw that pitch?"

Ellie's disarming voice and the glow of the wine put Tommy in an introspective mood. "I really don't know," he said, looking Ellie straight in the face. "It just happens."

"What do you mean, 'it just happens'?"

"I don't know how I learned it. It's like a gift."

Ellie flashed a puzzled smile. "That's crazy. You must be doing something different in your windup or your grip. That pitch defies the laws of physics."

"I'm not doing much. I just grab the ball and let it fly." Tommy lowered his head. "I ask myself all the time, how did this happen?"

Ellie wrapped her arm around Tommy's shoulders. "Don't question yourself. Just enjoy the gift you've got." She planted a kiss on his lips.

"I guess guilt comes with the gift," he said. "I swear, I was almost out of baseball."

"You see that sunset out there," Ellie said, pointing to the horizon. "That's a gift too. Gifts from God come in many different forms. Everyone receives gifts, yours is just quite unusual. Cherish it."

Tommy held Ellie tight. "This date with you is certainly a gift," he said, kissing her passionately.

"I still can't believe I won the contest," Ellie said, softly grabbing his hand. "Maybe it was fate."

They lay back in the grass, and Ellie snuggled close, her thick brown hair spilling over Tommy's face. Before long, the roll of thunder could be heard in the distance. Clouds moved in and a warm summer shower started to fall. The two raced to the car fifty yards away, in competition to see who would get there first. Ellie bumped him on the way, laughing as she sought the advantage.

"You're not going anywhere. I've got the keys," he reminded her.

The rain started to fall harder. Tommy fiddled with the keys and unlocked the car remotely as he ran.

"Hurry! I'm getting soaked," Ellie called out.

"It's open. Hop in." They piled in the front seat, both out of breath.

Tommy handed his date a towel he spotted in the back seat. Ellie looked wet, but beautiful—fresh and natural. He kissed her again before they began the drive back to Macon.

When Tommy turned on the car radio, Alan Jackson's "Gone Country" came on. "That guy is from my hometown, Newnan," he said proudly. "They painted a mural of him on a building downtown."

Tommy and Ellie sat close and hummed along to their favorite songs on the radio as they drove home. Their musical tastes were similarly eclectic, running the gamut from country to rock and hip-hop, and they talked about the concerts they'd been to.

When the two arrived back in Macon, Tommy showed Ellie his apartment. Even the claustrophobic "broom closet" couldn't deter her from staying the night.

CHAPTER 10

No-hitters in Single-A baseball hardly raise an eyebrow, but back-to-back gems are bound to draw the attention of the parent club. In Atlanta, Braves Manager Whitey Showalter and General Manager Steve Bailey met in Showalter's office to discuss Tommy Browning's immediate future.

"I say we bring him right up to the big leagues. The kid's a phenom, and he can help us nail down a wild card," Bailey said.

As was often the case, the Braves had talent but were underachieving. A National League playoff berth was far from certain.

"Don't you think that's pushing him—a jump from Single-A to the majors? In all of my thirty-five years in baseball, I've never seen that," Showalter said.

"But this kid is dominating. He's being wasted in Macon," Bailey argued. "Plus he'll help attendance. He'll put fannies in the seats."

Showalter frowned and dusted off some baseball history. "You may be too young to remember this, Steve, but there was once a phenom named David Clyde, a left-handed pitcher. The Texas Rangers drafted him Number One and rushed him to the majors just twenty days after he'd pitched his last high-school game. The kid was only eighteen.

"They did it to boost attendance because they were in financial trouble," Showalter continued. "Well, Clyde wasn't ready for the bigs and it showed. Then he lost his confidence. His career was over by age twenty-six."

"I get your point, but Browning's twenty-one and been playing pro baseball for three years," the general manager said.

"It's still pushing it."

"But he's been dominating. I hear he's developed a dominant pitch. And we certainly need more starting pitching to get over the finish line."

"I know, I agree," Showalter said.

"And Browning could be the spark we need. I tell you, I'm hearing amazing stuff about this kid."

"It feels like we're rushing him," Showalter repeated.

The conversation hit pause while the two men mulled over the situation. Bailey could tell Showalter was intrigued but not quite sold.

"I tell you what, let's send our two best scouts to Macon to take a good look," Bailey said. "I'll tell Concannon to pitch him five innings so they get a solid appraisal and can put the radar gun on him. They tell me he hit 97 in his last game."

"Yeah, I heard that. But I want Rosen and Sanchez to verify it. Some of these speed guns are way off."

Bailey nodded, but his enthusiasm hardly waned. "This is the best way to help the club," he said. "I've been looking, but there aren't any quality pitchers on the market. Too many teams think they're still in the wild-card race. That goes for the American League too."

Showalter's face softened. "Okay, I'm on board. Let's see what the scouts say."

CHAPTER 11

Atlanta Braves scouts Stu Rosen and Chico Sanchez settled into their seats behind home plate at Luther Williams Field, hoping to be impressed.

"I'll wait until the third or fourth inning to use this," Sanchez said, raising up the radar gun. "That will give him time to get loose."

"Good. From what they're saying, Browning should be throwing smoke by then," Rosen replied.

"I hope so," Sanchez said, with a sly smile. "I asked Concannon not to tell him he was only going five innings. I want him thinking it's just another start. We'll see how his velocity is when he's pacing himself to go nine."

But it hardly looked like "just another start." The stadium was filling up quickly. Fans jumped to their feet and danced as the PA system blasted out "La Bamba" during warm-ups.

Sanchez tapped his notepad on his knee. "Always liked this song," he said, leaning over to bump shoulders with his fellow scout.

The PA announcer broke in after the Ritchie Valens classic completed its final bouncy chords. "Welcome to Luther Williams Field for tonight's *sellout* game"—she emphasized the word since Macon hadn't had one in years—"between the Winston-Salem Dash and *your* Macon Peaches."

The crowd response was deafening—by minor-league standards. The fans were hoping to see Tommy accomplish the impossible, a third straight no-hitter. He had an advantage going in since Winston-Salem had never faced Tommy in his new incarnation as the Browning Rifle. Tommy was fired up as he took the mound. He looked up in the stands and blew Ellie Wainwright a kiss.

"Don't overthrow," Bucky Beavers warned him, sensing his pitcher's adrenaline rush. "Just let it come naturally like you have been."

The first Dash batter took a strike before trying to bunt for a base hit. He fouled it off and eventually went down on strikes. The second batter tried to bunt too, but fared no better. Then Winston-Salem hitters tried taking short, choppy swings, similar to fast-pitch softball. Tommy could see from how the Dash approached the game that his reputation had already spread like wildfire throughout the league.

But nothing seemed to work for Winston-Salem as he piled up strikeouts. By the fourth inning, the Dash were still without a hit and had whiffed eight times.

The stadium organist began following strikeouts with the musical refrain from Queen's "Another One Bites the Dust."

A third straight no-hitter? To the fans, it seemed entirely possible.

Even from their seats, the two Braves scouts could see a pitch that defied explanation. "What in the world do you call that, a knuckle fastball?" Rosen said, clearly amazed.

Sanchez pushed the gun in front of his cohort. It read ninety-eight miles per hour. "And that ninety-eight comes in the final thirty feet before the ball reaches home plate," he said, shaking his head in disbelief.

Tommy ran off the field after the top of the fifth inning with Macon ahead 3–0. His final pitching line: no hits, three walks, ten strikeouts.

Concannon greeted his ace at the top steps of the dugout. "Great job, Tommy. Have a seat."

Tommy put on his warm-up jacket and sat in the corner of the dugout by himself. No one came near him.

When the top of the sixth arrived, Macon had built its lead to 5–0. Tommy jogged out of the dugout to take the mound.

"Where's he going?" yelled Concannon, looking over at Skeeter.

"Didn't you tell him he's coming out?" Skeeter asked.

"I told you to tell him!"

"Daggumit. I must not've heard ya."

Skeeter reluctantly trotted out to the mound, where Tommy had already taken a warm-up pitch. "Tommy, you're only supposed to go five today," Skeeter said sheepishly. "I thought you knew."

"What? Nobody told me that and I've got a no-hitter going."

"I know, but it's orders from above. We're trying to protect your arm."

After a moment of hesitation, infielders were starting to approach the mound to see what was going on.

"It's not my decision," Skeeter said before patting Tommy on the back and prying the ball from his hand. Skeeter was immediately showered with boos. The crowd didn't understand the quick hook any more than Tommy did.

A chant broke out in the stands: "Let Tommy pitch! Let Tommy pitch!" The organist tried to silence the revolt by playing "Don't Worry, Be Happy."

Skeeter dropped the ball on the mound and broke into a sprint to get off the field. "He's pitching a no-hitter! How can you take him out, you idiot?" yelled a guy from the box seats. Plastic bottles and balled-up aluminum foil from hot dog wrappers began raining down onto the field.

"Sure glad we didn't have that bobblehead giveaway tonight," Ziggy Dale remarked in the dugout, to no one in particular.

Tommy stormed off in a huff, but waved to the crowd and tipped his hat en route to the dugout. He was greeted by bench players, who were just as surprised.

"Who do you want in, Davey?" asked Skeeter, from the protection of the dugout. "I think they want to lynch me out there."

"Jackson. If he's not loose, he'll have to warm up on the mound."

But by the time Malcolm Jackson reached the field the fans had exited in droves. The ballpark was practically empty.

Concannon shook his head as the few remaining fans continued the Tommy chant throughout the game. "There's going to be hell to pay when the media get at us," he said to Skeeter.

Concannon was right. Even though the Peaches held on to win 6–4, the press demanded answers for the fans. Reporters rushed to the manager's office immediately after the last out was recorded and echoed the fans' displeasure. "Was Tommy Browning hurt?" asked a reporter from the *Macon Telegraph*. "Why would you take him out when he had a third straight no-hitter going?"

Concannon rubbed the back of his neck. "No, he's not hurt," he said hesitantly. "It was a baseball decision."

A sportswriter from the *Atlanta Journal-Constitution*, attending the game on the chance that history would be made again, immediately jumped in. "What does that mean?"

"Well, I can't say any more yet."

"Does that mean it came from orders up top?" the *AJC* reporter fired back.

"All I can say is Browning is being evaluated, thanks to his recent success."

The Macon reporter jumped back in. "For a promotion?"

Concannon squirmed a little more. "We'll see," he said with a smile.

"Davey, how come you let him go out to start the sixth before pulling him?"

"That was just a miscommunication."

The reporters and a local TV crew quickly moved on to interview Tommy, who had just emerged from the showers. He couldn't supply many answers either.

"Skeeter just told me it wasn't his decision," the pitcher muttered.

Tommy threw his clothes on before leaving the clubhouse. Ellie was outside to meet him. "Another great game," she said, giving him a big hug and a kiss. "I can't believe they pulled you."

"I can't either, Ellie," Tommy said, kicking the dirt. "I still got the win, but I was pretty pissed not to finish."

Ellie gave Tommy a mournful look, and not just because he was denied the chance for an unprecedented third straight no-hitter.

CHAPTER 12

Before practice the next day, a steady stream of teammates dropped by Tommy's clubhouse cubicle to rub elbows with their ace pitcher.

"You were awesome last night, man," Bucky said, delivering a high-five. "You're unhittable these days. I've never seen anything like it."

"So, why did they take me out?" Tommy asked. "Do you know anything about that?"

The catcher just shrugged. "I'm in the dark on that, too."

Davey Concannon soon provided the answer, delivering news that was part shocking, part joyous, and part bittersweet.

"Congratulations, Tommy, you're getting a promotion."

Tommy's smile stretched from ear to ear. "To Gwinnett?" he asked, hoping to jump Double-A for the Braves' Triple-A affiliate.

"Close. You won't be far away," the manager said coyly. "Son, you've been called up to The Show. The Braves want you with them today."

Tommy screamed so loud, every player in the clubhouse turned around.

"I know you don't have a car, and you can't take Ziggy's again. The Braves will send a driver to get you."

Tommy grabbed his manager in a bear hug. "This is unbelievable. I'm going to the big leagues!"

Immediately, teammates began swarming around Tommy while Concannon jumped back so he wouldn't get trampled.

Most offered congratulations with a tinge of jealousy in their voices. From Single-A ball straight to the major leagues, it sounded like the impossible dream.

"Man, you have got to tell me your secret," center fielder Levon Quick said. "About a month ago, we would have voted you the player most likely to be stocking shelves at Kroger next year."

"Drop my name to them when you get up there," Daryl Wilson, a first-baseman, said.

Bucky gave Tommy a hug. "The Browning Rifle's going big time. You think they want your personal catcher, too?"

Skeeter approached Concannon in the background. "Y'all know Browning became a superstar after I began working with him, right? Where's my promotion?"

"I'll let you know when they call, Skeeter." Concannon turned and shook his head as he approached Tommy again. "All right, guys, let's head out to practice. Not you, Tommy. You'd better get your things together. The driver will be here around four o'clock."

"Where am I going to stay tonight?"

"They'll probably put you up in a hotel until you can find an apartment in Atlanta. I guarantee you it won't be an Econo Lodge," Concannon said with a smirk.

Tommy pumped his fist upon hearing that. "Yes!"

"Just get your clothes and some essentials. You can pick up your other crap later."

"Do you think they will use me tonight against the Marlins? I mean, I just threw five innings last night."

The manager threw his hands up, appearing exasperated. "How the hell would I know? I don't know how it works. You think I've ever had a player go straight to the big leagues?"

Concannon paused before adding, "I never even made The Show myself. Be sure and tell me what it's like."

Hearing those words made Tommy appreciate the moment even more. It suddenly dawned on him that he was becoming the lucky one player in ten who realizes his dream.

"Go now and get back here before four. You can clean out your locker then," Concannon said, waving Tommy off. But he grabbed his overnight sensation by the arm before Tommy could go.

"Hey, good luck to you, son. We're all rooting for you."

Tommy stared wide-eyed through the window of the SUV as it pulled up to Truist Park. He'd never actually seen the modern ballpark before, which was surrounded by trendy restaurants and outdoor mall shopping, all designed to make the destination more than just a baseball game but an "experience."

The assistant general manager for the Braves stopped the vehicle and unclicked his seatbelt. "Welcome to the big leagues," he said to his passenger. Tommy rolled out of the SUV and immediately looked up at the majestic stadium, eager to become a Brave.

"Come on into my office and we'll have you sign the player's contract. Then we'll go see Whitey and Herb, the pitching coach."

Before the two men got to the office, they spotted Whitey Showalter in the hallway. He looked exactly like he did on TV— middle-aged, with a stomach paunch and his trademark shock of white hair.

"Heard great things about you, Tommy. They tell me you were tearing up Single-A," the manager said, shaking hands.

"What did you have, twenty-three straight hitless innings? If you can do that up here, we'll have to call you Cy Young."

Tommy smiled modestly as Showalter turned to the assistant GM. "I think old Cy once threw twenty-five straight hitless innings. That's the record."

"Do you want him in uniform tonight, Whitey?"

"Not necessary tonight. Game time's right around the corner. Just have Tommy sign a contract and get settled in a hotel. He can meet Herb tomorrow."

Tommy looked disappointed. He hoped to be in uniform that night, but it was already pushing six o'clock.

The assistant GM led Tommy into his office and explained the salary. "Under the new collective bargaining agreement between Major League Baseball and the Players' Union, when you're brought up to the majors for the first time and don't already have a major-league contract you get the standard minimum salary prorated. It works out to 1/183rd of the salary daily."

"How much is that?" Tommy asked.

"The minimum salary is now $700,000, so that works out to $3,825 per day."

Tommy was practically foaming at the mouth. He wanted to scream at the top of his lungs. "Did you say $3,825 a day?"

"That's right."

"And does it start today?"

"As soon as you sign the contract," the assistant GM replied.

"At that point, Tommy was ready to rip the pen out of the man's hand. "Where do I sign?" he asked.

"Right here, but look over the contract first."

The lookover took about ten seconds.

"Let me explain a few other standard agreements," the assistant GM said as Tommy scribbled down his name. "If you stay with our club for three years you'll be eligible for arbitration, and in four years you will qualify for free agency."

Arbitration and free agency were hardly of importance to Tommy at that moment. But the next words out of the assistant GM's mouth were.

"Why don't I take you to your hotel? By contract with the Players Association, we put you up at the Omni for up to four nights. It overlooks the ballpark. But I'd start looking for an apartment or living space as soon as possible. You shouldn't have any trouble. There are plenty of places to rent around here."

Tommy's mind flashed back to the "broom closet." He'd only traveled about ninety miles that day, but he was in a whole different universe.

That night Tommy was lying on his plush hotel room bed, gobbling down room service dinner and watching television. He let the phone ring five times before reluctantly picking it up.

"Hi mom," he said between bites of his filet mignon.

"Tommy, what's going on? We haven't heard from you in a week. I've been calling and texting you, but you never answer. Is everything all right?"

"Everything's great. I'm just too busy. I've been called up to the Braves. I'm at the Omni hotel."

"You what?" His mom nearly dropped the phone as she called out to her husband. "Harold, come quick. Tommy's been called up to the major leagues. Here, I'll put this on speaker phone."

"I knew they couldn't ignore you for long," his dad said, speaking loudly as he approached the phone from the living room. "Congratulations, son."

"Did you get a uniform?" Evelyn asked, breathlessly. She moved the phone between her and her husband.

"I get one tomorrow. And get this, I'll be making $3,825 a day."

Harold chimed in. "Wow! We're so proud of you, Tommy. I guess we were wrong. Maybe you didn't have to go to college after all."

"Yeah, I made the right call, that's for sure. Who needs education?" Tommy said. "Hey, I've got to go now. I'm real busy."

"You can't talk some more? We need to catch up." His mom sounded shocked.

"Not now. The, uh, Braves want to see me."

"Just get your proper rest and do what they say," Evelyn said.

"Yeah, yeah, don't worry."

Tommy tossed his phone onto the bed and finished his dinner. Then he headed down to the hotel bar. He couldn't wait to see what girls were hanging around, looking to snag a rising Braves star.

CHAPTER 13

The last twenty-four hours seemed like something from a dream, like Tommy had died and gone to heaven. He broke into a broad smile as he soaked in the intoxicating aura of the Braves clubhouse and dressed for a home game against the Miami Marlins. For the first time, he was putting on an Atlanta Braves uniform. He stared down at the embroidered tomahawk on the front and tapped it for good luck. Then he turned the jersey around and admired his name above the number "55."

One of his new teammates stopped by Tommy's cubicle to meet him. "Hey, rook, congratulations on the call," reliever Patrick Walker said. "I've heard good things about you, but remember, this ain't Single-A. Everybody can hit a fastball up here."

That icy skepticism seemed to pervade the clubhouse. Some of the players were aware of Tommy's fabled exploits through recent coverage in the *Atlanta Journal-Constitution*, but doubted that he could pitch on the highest professional level. Some resented the fact that he was being fast-tracked to the big leagues, skipping two levels of minor-league ball.

Other players wondered why the Braves would tinker with the roster when they were on such a roll. Riding an eight-game winning streak, Atlanta had just taken over first place in the National League East.

Plus, anytime a new player is brought up, someone on the roster has to be sent down or put on the Injured List to make room. That could create a touchy situation in the clubhouse where friendships come into play.

When Tommy was done dressing, he put on his hat with the big A, briefly admired himself in the small mirror mounted inside his cubicle, and waited for instructions. The Braves pitching coach, Herb Blasingame, stopped by to introduce himself—a little more cordially than Walker—and directed him to the left-field bullpen.

"Will I get in the game tonight?" Tommy asked eagerly.

"You never can tell," Blasingame said. "Always be ready, just in case."

Tommy left the clubhouse and walked slowly through the tunnel that led to the Braves dugout, taking care to pick up his cleats so he wouldn't lose his footing and slip. When he got outside, he afforded himself a minute to soak in the atmosphere: vendors hawking peanuts, the smell of freshly grilled hot dogs, and the buzz of the arriving crowd, which appeared close to a sellout. Unlike minor-league parks, anticipation filled the air. Anticipation of great things to come.

The stadium grass actually was greener than in the minor leagues, just like people said. And it was perfectly manicured. No bad hops to worry about.

As he strolled over the diamond to the bullpen, it dawned on Tommy that he was nine years old the last time he was in a major-league park, Atlanta's Turner Field. Never in his wildest childhood fantasies did he expect to be in Truist Park as a player for the Braves.

An old baseball expression came to mind: The game changes when they put on that second deck. He reminded himself of the formidable odds he overcame to rocket to the major leagues at age twenty-one. This was a moment to cherish.

Once he reached the bullpen, Tommy found himself in the

company of nearly ten other pitchers, some half expecting to play that night and others just hanging out or doing light throwing. The latter were in the starting rotation.

Many of the pitchers gave the newcomer awkward looks— not quite icy but wary just the same. Tommy nodded to a few but didn't get much of a response. Finally, a smiling Black man came up and shook his hand. Tommy didn't need an introduction. He knew all about Tyrone Barnwell.

Barnwell's pitching record was currently 15–5 with a 3.12 ERA. He was clearly the ace of the staff.

"How are you, Tommy? I heard you got called up."

Tommy was thrilled that Ty Barnwell knew his name. "I'm great, Ty," he said, trying to appear relaxed. He skootched over on the bench to give the star more room. "Thanks for asking. You're the first guy to actually say hello."

"Really? Don't worry, we've got a good group of guys. They'll warm to you once you've been here a while." He placed his hand on Tommy's shoulder. "I'm hearing good things about you, man. Heard you were slaying it in Single-A with no-hitters."

Tommy couldn't help but puff out his chest. "I developed a new pitch," he said.

"You'll have to show me how you throw it sometime," Barnwell said.

Tommy immediately regretted having said that.

After an awkward pause, Barnwell reignited the conversation. "I read you were a twenty-second-round pick. That's beating the odds."

Tommy was amazed that Ty Barnwell knew so much about him. His ego was growing by the minute.

"That's right. I stuck with baseball and it paid off. You were a high draft pick, weren't you?" Tommy knew full well the answer to that question. He just wanted to continue the conversation.

"Yeah, I was a first-rounder out of Vanderbilt. I started in Double-A but made it to the big leagues in three years."

"Same with me," Tommy quickly said. "I made it in three years too."

Barnwell looked surprised that Tommy appeared to be equating the career paths of the two. "There's a saying up here, man. Getting to the major leagues is the easy part. Staying here is the hard part."

Tommy nodded.

"Let me give you some tips," Barnwell said. "If you ever feel any unusual tweak or pain when you're throwing, tell Herb immediately, and he'll tell Whitey. You don't want to jeopardize your career by letting it get worse. That play-through-the-pain stuff goes out the window now that you're a pro. Hey, Curt Schilling became a Boston legend for pitching in the bloody sock, but you don't need to be. You've got to protect your career. You'll find out this is a business, if you haven't already. Do what's best for you."

Tommy nodded again. The advice seemed particularly relevant to the Browning Rifle.

"And another thing," Barnwell continued. "We play one hundred and sixty-two games. You have to be able to manage the highs and lows, because you'll have both. Over a long season, you may not stay healthy. You'll probably get arm trouble at some point. Most pitchers do. If you make it through a full big-league season with just stiffness, you're Superman. With all due respect to your no-hitters, another pitcher had to go on IL, or to the minors, for you to be brought up. That was Ramirez. His arm's dead."

Barnwell got up to do some stretching, but later returned to watch the game. After six innings, the Braves were comfortably ahead of the Marlins 8–1 and seemed well on their way to a ninth straight win.

In the dugout, manager Showalter reached for the bullpen phone.

"Herb, why don't we give our call-up, Browning, an inning?" he said into the phone.

"I thought we were going to use him as a starter?" replied the pitching coach, clearly surprised.

"I know, but this is a good chance for him to get his feet wet. There's no pressure. We've got a big lead. I'm dying to see what he's got."

"Browning just pitched a couple of days ago."

"I know, and I still plan to start him. But even though we're hearing glowing reports, he *is* making an awfully big jump. Maybe this will allow him to work out the jitters, and if he does well we can start him in the series with the Mets."

Blasingame wasn't going to buck the manager. "Okay, I'll get him up to throw."

"Have him pitch the eighth. That will give him time to get loose. Let our eighth-inning guy throw the ninth and give Walker a rest. That's unless all hell breaks loose."

"Sure thing, Whitey," Blasingame said, hanging up the bullpen phone. He trotted over to inform Tommy. "Go get loose, Tommy. You're pitching the eighth."

Tommy sprang to his feet, a bit in shock. "Where's my glove?" he stammered, looking around.

"It fell behind the bench," Barnwell said with a laugh. He tossed the glove to his new teammate, who dropped it. Seeing that, Barnwell rose from the bench, grabbed the glove off the ground, and slowly handed it to Tommy.

"Just go out and enjoy this," he said, draping his arm around the rookie. "Throw strikes and don't shake off the catcher. If you don't walk people, you'll be fine."

Tommy nodded and proceeded to the practice mound, where the bullpen catcher was waiting. It dawned on him that this was mop-up relief, just like that night against Greenville when he saved his career. But this was the major leagues and his team was ahead. Certainly, there was no shame in being a mop-up man.

After eight pitches, Tommy was loose and started to throw harder. That's when panic began to set in. His trick fastball wasn't moving. The speed didn't change from butterfly to bullet like it normally did. The pitch came in straight, and not very fast. Where was the violent pounding sound from the catcher's glove?

Soon Blasingame alerted Tommy that it was the top of the eighth and Tommy began the anxious walk through the gate onto the outfield grass.

"How'd he look, Gus?" Blasingame asked his bullpen catcher.

Gus shook his head slowly. "Well, he's got a pretty decent curveball, but that fastball didn't have much pop. It could have been that he was holding back, though."

"How about his mystery pitch?"

"I never saw it," said Gus, throwing up his hands.

When Tommy got to the mound, he took a few more warm-up pitches that also lacked magic. Catcher Hal Bagley wasn't impressed, so he trotted out to see him.

"You're starting out with the cleanup hitter, a real good stick. You need to move the ball around to wherever I put my glove. And don't get behind in the count or he'll sit on your fastball."

Bagley slapped Tommy on the rear with his catcher's glove before jogging back behind home plate.

"Now pitching for the Braves, Tommy Browning," announced a voice over the public address system. A generous round of applause only added to Tommy's anxiety.

This is what I've been working for, he told himself. *Don't blow it.*

The Marlins batter took a curveball low before ripping the next pitch into the left-centerfield alley for a double.

"Welcome to the big leagues," mumbled Bagley from behind his mask.

As the next batter stepped in, Tommy got the call for a fastball again. He simply grabbed the baseball and let it rip, almost pleading to the ball as it left his hand, like a man in search of a miracle.

This time the ball fluttered for a second or two before exploding to home plate. Bagley was so startled, he appeared handcuffed and managed just to knock the ball down.

"Strike one," called out the ump, as the batter dropped his bat in disbelief.

Before long, the Browning Rifle had fanned the side. In doing so, he made three veteran major-league hitters look like bush leaguers.

"Hey, Herb," yelled Gus in the bullpen. "I guess he *was* holding back."

Just then the bullpen phone rang. "Herb, I've seen enough," Whitey Showalter said, his words rushing out. "I want Browning to start the third game against the Mets."

CHAPTER 14

Five days later, play-by-play man Ken Allen and color analyst Freddy Feld worked the television broadcast booth as the Braves hosted the Mets to end the home stand.

Allen: "Tonight, the fans get to see the first major-league start for heralded rookie Tommy Browning, Freddy."

Feld: "Yes, we're all excited to see what the Browning Rifle can do, Ken. His rise has been nothing short of phenomenal."

Allen: "What does Browning have to do to beat the Mets, Freddy?"

Feld: "Stay in his zone and not get rattled. We haven't seen him struggle yet, so we don't know how he'll react. I'm sure the Mets will step out of the box, mess with his rhythm, and maybe even lay down a few bunts."

Allen: "Try to get the Browning Rifle to misfire?"

Feld: "You might say that. We'll see if he has the ammunition to mow down a good-hitting lineup."

Allen: "Browning fanned three in his impressive debut a few nights back, but as a starter he could face each player in the lineup three or four times before the bullpen takes over. That's a real challenge."

Feld: "You got that right. Good hitters make adjustments."

Allen: "We'll be back with the starting lineups after this break. The Braves try to start another win streak after losing 5–4 to the Mets last night. Don't go away."

First Inning

Allen: "A called strike three. Two down in the top of the first as Browning has his fastball—or magic pitch—working."

Feld: "In all my years as a player and broadcaster, I've never seen anything like it, Ken. The scouting reports were right. It starts like a Phil Niekro knuckleball and ends like a Nolan Ryan fastball."

Fourth Inning

Allen: "And the Braves now stretch their lead to 4–0 on the two-run triple by Carlos Lagares. Lagares can really fly. That's his third triple of the season."

Feld: "He's faster than a fat man to a buffet."

Allen: "The way Browning is throwing, this could be more than enough runs to get him his first major-league win, Freddy. He's looked in total control."

Feld: "Like a shark at a fish fry."

Sixth Inning

Allen: "That's Tommy Browning's seventh strikeout, and he still has not allowed a hit."

Feld: "Incredible. The Mets have all batted against him at least twice. They look baffled. It seems like their best chance is to hit the curveball, which he sneaks in now and then."

Allen: "But three-quarters of his pitches have been that crazy fastball. It's not too early to think no-hitter."

Feld: "He's still got to get through the lineup a third time, and the hitters may get more comfortable now that they've seen him twice. But yeah, I think he's got a shot at it."

Allen: "And making history. I've just been handed this

from the Braves' public relations staff. Browning is bidding to become the first pitcher to throw a no-hitter in his initial big-league start since Tyler Gilbert of the Arizona Diamondbacks in 2021. Before that, only three other pitchers have done that: Bobo Holloman of the St. Louis Browns in 1953, Bumpus Jones of the Cincinnati Reds in 1892, and Ted Breitenstein for the Browns in 1891. By the way, the Browns became the Baltimore Orioles."

Feld: "I didn't know that."

Allen: "They relocated to Baltimore after the 1953 season. Bobo Holloman gave St. Louis a thrill before the team left town."

Eighth Inning

Allen: "We'd like to welcome back our viewers after that commercial break. The Braves lead the New York Mets 4–0, and Tommy Browning has been superb. He's six outs away from pitching a no-hitter in his first major-league start."

Feld: "He's got the bottom of the order: seven, eight, and nine. This inning shouldn't be a problem."

Allen: "Smith goes down swinging. He's now five outs away. Up comes Travis McGarry, a left-handed hitter. He lays off a high fastball and the count runs to 3–1."

Feld: "One of the few times Browning has been behind in the count all night. Javier Soto is in a step at third, guarding against a bunt."

Allen: "McGarry takes a late swing and hits a grounder between short and third. It gets through! A single breaks up the no-hitter!"

Feld: "What a shame. That ball had eyes."

Allen: "Browning slaps his glove against his leg in disappointment."

In the clubhouse afterward, reporters swarmed around Tommy's locker. The rookie had just thrown a one-hit shutout in his first major-league start.

"Tommy, how disappointing was it to lose the no-hitter in the eighth?"

"It sucks," Tommy said without a thought that his comment would be quoted in the paper.

"But you still got a complete-game shutout for your first major-league win," a radio reporter interjected. "You've got to be happy with that. That ball barely made it through the infield."

Tommy gave the reporter a cold stare. "Yeah, well, Soto was a little slow to react. I've played with other third basemen who would have had it."

The reporters looked stunned over the frank response. They soon dispersed to make evening deadlines.

Two stalls down, Javier Soto was sitting next to Lagares, swaying to salsa music on the radio. Lagares overheard Tommy's comments and translated them in Spanish to Soto, who hailed from the Dominican Republic and spoke very little English. Soto jumped to his feet. He turned angrily and shouted at Tommy in Spanish: "Nadie podria haber llegado a esa bola, estupido bastardo."

"What did he say?" Tommy asked in a disgusted voice.

Lagares paused. He knew what Soto had said: *No one could have reached that ball, you stupid bastard.* Instead he said with a playful smile, "He said you pitched a great game. He wishes he could have made the play."

Tommy stared back at Soto. "I do too, man," he said.

Soto shouted again in Spanish. "No me culpe. Hice lo mejor que pude." *Don't blame me. I did my best.*

Lagares turned to Tommy again. "Javier says he got a bad jump on the ball, but he'll get it next time."

Tommy returned a wry smile.

Soto grumbled something under his breath: "Usted es solo un novato arrogante."

Lagares laughed and looked back at Tommy one last time. "He says you are a great man."

But Tommy didn't know what he'd really said: *You are just an arrogant rookie.*

CHAPTER 15

Early the next morning, Lew Edwards did a double-take before dropping the sports section of the *Atlanta Journal-Constitution* and getting up from his desk inside Edwards BMW.

"I'll take this one, Bill," he said to his sales associate. "Can I help you?" Lew said, hurrying out to greet the customer.

"Yes sir. Y'all got some used BMWs I can look at?" Tommy inquired.

"Aren't you Tommy Browning from the Braves? I saw the game last night on TV."

"Yeah, it's me, all right," Tommy said, looking around the showroom.

The salesman shook his hand. "Wow, you almost pitched a no-hitter last night. If it wasn't for that one little ground ball . . ."

Tommy winced. "I know, I know. Hey, you have any used cars around here?"

Edwards continued to stare at Tommy as Tommy surveyed the showroom. Finally, he broke out of his trance. "We don't deal in used cars, Tommy. But I can give you a sweet deal on one of the cars in stock—that's why they call me Sweet Lew. We're moving them out before next year's models arrive."

"Wow, that's pretty early," Tommy said. "It's only September."

"Everything moves fast in the luxury car business," Lew replied.

Tommy spotted a shiny white model and jumped in, admiring the dashboard while Edwards rattled off some of the features.

"You can take it for a test drive if you want. This is our 2 Series Gran Coupe. It's a beautiful car and priced to move."

Tommy hesitated after spotting the sticker price—over $35,000. Lew could tell by the look on his face that Tommy had never purchased a new car before. The salesman recognized sticker shock when he saw it.

"I . . . uh . . . don't know if this is in my price range, but I guess it doesn't hurt to test-drive it."

"Not at all," said the salesman. "I'll get the keys and be right back."

After test-driving on the highway and the streets of Alpharetta, Tommy looked smitten. "That sure is a sweet ride," he said, his eyes glued on the vehicle. "But I still don't know if I can afford it."

"Let me crunch some numbers and we'll know," Edwards said, leading Tommy into his office. He stopped midway and turned back to his customer. "After seeing you pitch last night, I think you're going to have a long career in the major leagues."

Tommy thought about that. He was already earning nearly four grand a day, and next year he'd be pulling in a minimum of $700,000 if he pitched well enough to stay with the Braves.

He didn't need much more convincing. Edwards knocked a few thousand dollars off the price, accepted a small down payment, and worked out a financing plan. In less than an hour, Tommy owned an ostentatious set of wheels.

"But there's one more part to the deal," Edwards said.

Tommy frowned. "What's that?" he asked with skepticism.

"I want you to autograph a baseball for me."

Tommy arrived at the ballpark that day in love with life. He had found an apartment in the upper-crusty Buckhead section of Atlanta, and in a day or two he would be driving a new BMW.

But when Whitey Showalter spotted him entering the clubhouse, the manager immediately pulled Tommy into his office.

"First of all, you pitched a helluva game last night, Tommy. I want to congratulate you on that. Bagley said the movement on your pitches was out of this world."

Tommy straightened up proudly upon hearing the rave review.

"It's the stuff after the game that concerns me. You blamed our third baseman for the hit. That's not the way big-league players act. You don't criticize teammates."

Tommy looked away. He couldn't think of anything to say in his defense.

"Now I know it was a disappointment to lose the no-hitter, and I think you kept your composure pretty good on the field, especially for a twenty-one-year-old. That's why I let you finish the game. It told me something about you." Tommy looked Showalter in the eyes again.

"However," said Showalter, "the media took your post-game remarks and ran with 'em." He passed over his copy of the *Journal-Constitution* so Tommy could see. The headline read: "Rookie Browning barely misses no-hitter"

The subhead below it read: "Blames Soto for not getting to ground ball"

"That's not a good look for the organization. And it wasn't just them. TV stations aired your words on tape."

Tommy stayed silent and passed the newspaper back to his manager.

"We've got good chemistry on this team, Tommy. Don't

upset the applecart. Don't criticize your teammates, and watch what you say to the media."

Showalter sighed as he stuffed the newspaper away under some scouting reports. "Now go get dressed and head on out to batting practice. I've got to work on tonight's lineup card. Congratulations on your first major-league win."

"Thanks, Skip. I'll remember what you said." But as Tommy walked away, he still harbored a slight grudge toward Soto. He was just being too honest.

For a starter, the day after pitching basically consisted of stretching, jogging, outfield sprints, easy tossing, and maybe lifting a few light weights. But sudden stardom made Tommy's day a little different. When he took the field, he was besieged by fans hanging over the box seats, clamoring for his autograph.

"Tommy, Tommy, please sign, please sign!" came the impassioned pleas.

He ignored both kids and adults alike, walking right past them without breaking stride. But there was one person standing alone down the third baseline whom he couldn't ignore.

"Hey hotshot, remember me?" Ellie Wainwright looked at Tommy through mirrored sunglasses. She took them off to show her full face.

Tommy stopped in his tracks. "Hi Ellie. What brings you here?" He immediately regretted the stupid response.

"How come you never called me, not even to say goodbye?" Ellie's voice was tinged with anger. "I thought I meant something to you."

"Sorry, I, uh . . . I got called up so fast. Everything's been happening so fast."

"You couldn't even call?"

Tommy was silent.

"I knew you wouldn't be in Macon long. Ballplayers come and go. But you're still nearby."

"Ellie, I've just been very busy."

"I haven't heard from you in over a month. Maybe we haven't been going out long, but I thought we were a couple."

Tommy impulsively shot a glance toward the other pitchers, who were starting to stretch in the outfield grass.

"I gotta go," he said, jogging away. "Good to see you again, Ellie."

Tommy's urgent departure to stretch was abruptly interrupted less than forty feet away when a buxom blonde dressed in short shorts caught his attention down the left-field line. The woman leaned over the railing in her low-cut halter top, revealing ample cleavage.

Ellie watched in horror as Tommy lingered and eventually signed her breasts with a felt marker. The woman passed him a piece of paper, which he stuffed in the back pocket of his baseball pants.

Ellie shook her head in disgust as she watched Tommy give the woman a spirited thumbs-up before departing. "Well, bless your little heart," Ellie called out, sarcastically.

Tommy never broke stride and never looked back.

CHAPTER 16

About a week later, reliever Patrick Walker approached Tommy in the clubhouse and plopped down in a chair next to him. "One of the guys told me they saw you pull into the ballpark in a new BMW with a hot blonde in the car," he said.

Tommy smiled, proud that he'd been noticed. "That's right. Her name's Candy."

"Is she your new squeeze?"

"We've been out a couple of times," Tommy replied, reaching into his locker for some hand lotion. "Had a great time Thursday night. We went out to the movies and then she came back to my apartment for drinks."

"Oh, yeah? Did you get her to spend the night?"

Tommy returned a sly smile but didn't say anything.

"Where'd you meet her?"

"At the ballpark. She's a fan."

"Did she tell you what she does for a living?"

Tommy was growing suspicious of Walker's interest. Did he want to steal his Candy away? He abruptly turned and looked for something in his locker. "She's a dancer," he said. "Why are you so interested?"

Walker stood from his chair and moved in closer. "Just thought you'd like to know, a bunch of the guys have been with her too, including myself. She's a stripper at the Pussy Cat Lounge in Atlanta. Her stage name is Candy Samples."

Tommy looked stunned.

"She's a ballpark groupie, a Baseball Annie. You know they're out there."

Tommy sat in silence, trying not to react. He thought Candy wanted him exclusively, and he never thought she was a stripper.

Walker slapped him on the shoulder before strolling away. "I just thought you'd want to know, that's all."

Tommy continued to pitch well in his starts following the one-hitter, but there were signs that his cloak of invincibility was starting to fray. Major-league hitters were making contact more often, adjusting to the sudden acceleration of his fastball. Most still swung late, but they were increasingly putting the ball in play.

Still, he raised his pitching record to 3–0 with a pair of five-hitters. Neither were complete games as Showalter limited Tommy to seven innings, wanting to give his bullpen work.

The fans and media were still enthralled with the Browning Rifle. A newspaper columnist even floated a name for his mystery pitch: the Tommy Gun.

Tommy showed no real signs of slowing down, but that didn't stop Herb Blasingame from approaching him one Monday, an off day, in the bullpen. "I'm going to teach you something that will make you unhittable again," the pitching coach promised.

"I'm all ears," Tommy replied.

"I know you don't throw a changeup, and I can't for the life of me understand why," Blasingame said. "You've got a fastball that explodes late. A changeup would be the perfect complement—a pitch that appears to be a fastball before the bottom drops out. It would really screw up the batter's timing, which is what every pitcher wants."

Tommy looked entranced with the thought, staring off into space.

"Have you ever tried to throw a changeup?" Blasingame asked, grabbing a baseball.

"Not really," Tommy answered.

"I guess nobody had time to teach you, you shot up to the big leagues so fast," Blasingame said with a laugh.

Tommy wanted to remind him that he'd spent two-and-a-half years languishing in Single-A.

Blasingame placed the baseball in Tommy's right hand. "There are some variations of the grip, but let's start with this one. Spread these two middle fingers over the seam with the thumb underneath the ball. Keep the ball back in your hand. It's a deeper grip than the fastball."

Tommy allowed him to move his fingers around the ball just so.

"Now it's very important that you throw the ball with consistent arm-speed, the same as a fastball. That helps disguise it," he added. "Try throwing some to Gus."

After getting loose, Tommy threw some changeups to the bullpen catcher while Blasingame watched over his shoulder.

"You're getting there," Blasingame said. "What you're looking for is a pitch that's 10 to 12 percent slower than your fastball. But for you, the way your fastball pops, it might even be more."

Blasingame yelled to his bullpen catcher. "What are you seeing, Gus?"

"It's running and sinking some," he reported.

"You're not going to get it perfect in one day," Blasingame

said. "You can try some different variations on the grip. Here, I'll show you some."

After demonstrating grips and staying another fifteen minutes, Blasingame looked at his watch. "I've got to go meet with Whitey and the GM," he said. "Work on the pitch whenever you have time, but that's probably enough for today. I don't want you to get a sore arm."

Blasingame started to walk away, but he suddenly stopped and looked back at his student. "There's a saying in baseball: Hitting is about timing and pitching is about messing up timing. Always remember that."

Tommy thanked the pitching coach for his help. Now he might have a third pitch to go with the mystery fastball and a pretty good curveball. And three pitches are practically a necessity in the major leagues.

When Blasingame entered Showalter's office the general manager, Bailey, was already talking playoffs.

"It looks like we're going to play the Brewers in the National League Division Series, who we match up well against," Bailey pointed out. "That's assuming we win the NL East, but with a six-game lead now, I think we're pretty safe."

"Wait a minute, Steve, don't jinx us," Showalter said.

Bailey returned a confident smile. "I think we can go places. We're really jelling after the slow start, and the addition of Browning gives us another stopper to go with Barnwell. Plus, Anderson's capable of throwing a shutout on any given day."

Showalter turned to Blasingame. "We'll have to map out a playoff rotation, Herb, or see if we're better off using a lot of arms for a few innings each."

"I don't think that would be wise, Whitey, especially now

that we've added Browning to the roster. He can dominate, and if he ever gets down the changeup I've been teaching him, watch out."

"How do you think he'll react to playoff pressure?" Showalter asked.

Blasingame shrugged. "There's no way of telling, Whitey. Not until he gets out there."

"So true," Showalter said with a nod.

"But one thing Browning has going for him: the Brewers, Dodgers, and Giants haven't seen him yet."

"Good point," Showalter said. "Wait till they see that screwy fastball of his."

Bailey jumped back in. "We need to finalize the playoff roster in the next week."

Showalter leaned back in his recliner. "Unless somebody gets hurt, we're standing pat, Steve. We've got a lot of good arms and a solid lineup one through nine. I think the Atlanta Braves are going to be heard from this year."

CHAPTER 17

Hal Bagley was brimming with confidence as he took his position behind home plate for Game 2 of the National League Divisional Series. The Braves had won Game 1 against the Milwaukee Brewers, 3–0, behind the pitching of ace Ty Barnwell, and they had the Browning Rifle on the mound for Game 2.

Bagley could tell Tommy had his good stuff. The ball was dancing and exploding in warm-ups. Out of the corner of his eye he could see the Milwaukee bench studying Browning, a collective look of disbelief on their faces.

As so often was the case when a team saw Tommy for the first time, the Brewers were tentative at the plate, taking a lot of pitches.

"They must be hoping he'll walk them," Bagley told Showalter between innings. "That ain't gonna happen."

From the dugout, Brewers manager Max Shoenstein watched Tommy intently. A man who had spent fifty years in professional baseball, he couldn't believe his eyes and was about to do something about it.

Milwaukee picked up its first hit on a bunt single in the top of the third but trailed 1–0. When Tommy struck out his fifth batter with the Tommy Gun, Shoenstein had seen enough.

"Time," he called out before approaching the home-plate umpire. The ump pulled off his mask and looked annoyed at the delay.

"I want you to check the ball and his glove," Shoenstein said.

"Oh, come on, Ump. Our pitcher's legit. They just can't hit him," Bagley grumbled.

The umpire called for the ball from Tommy, twirled it around in his hand to examine it, and threw it back to the pitcher. "The ball is fine," he said.

"Well, let's examine his glove," Shoenstein said. "I swear he's doing something to the baseball."

The ump shrugged and walked out to the pitcher's mound. That brought Whitey Showalter out too.

Taking the glove from Tommy, the home-plate umpire was now joined by two other umps from the first and third baselines, plus the entire Braves infield. The meeting at the mound was growing so fast it began to resemble a summit meeting on global warming.

The home-plate umpire seemed satisfied with the outside of the glove, but when he put his hand inside his demeanor changed.

"What's this greasy stuff in the fingers?"

Tommy grabbed the glove back. "That's just hand lotion. I use it because my hands get dry."

The ump didn't want to hear an explanation. He threw up his arm and ejected Tommy. "That's a foreign substance on your glove. It's against the rules."

The full house at Truist Park rained down boos as Showalter pushed his way in front of the ump. "You can't throw my pitcher out for that!"

"I just did, Whitey."

"Well, we're playing this game under protest."

Tommy was stunned, too stunned to even argue. He started to jog off the field and head into the dugout, but the third-base umpire caught up to him and confiscated his glove.

"You can't stay in the dugout. You need to go in the club-house," the ump said.

"Why are you taking my glove?"

"The league office needs to examine it for illicit grip aids," the ump replied.

Tommy shook his head in disgust. He watched the rest of the game on TV in the Braves' clubhouse.

Showalter was visibly agitated and pushed his argument but stopped short of being thrown out of the game. This was the playoffs; he needed to be around.

Jerome Wheeler took the mound to replace Tommy. After his warm-up pitches, Bagley visited him on the mound. "I want you to throw some chin music to Mason this inning, just to send a message. They had no reason to get Browning tossed."

"Did Whitey say to do that?" Wheeler asked.

"Don't worry, Whitey will be fine with it. Don't hit him, just brush him back."

Wheeler nodded. "One bow tie coming up," he said.

"And keep the runner close," Bagley added before returning to home plate.

Wheeler brushed back Mason with a high and tight fastball, leading to some howling from the Milwaukee bench. But Mason wasn't intimidated. He dug in and stroked an RBI double to tie the game 1–1.

In the clubhouse, there was no one to hear Tommy complain but the equipment manager. "That was freakin' hand cream. How can they throw me out for that?"

"You got me. I just work here," the equipment manager replied.

The run was charged to Tommy, but Wheeler shut the door after that with five scoreless innings before Walker closed in a

2–1 Braves victory. Bagley's solo home run in the eighth was the difference.

Bagley attended the post-game press conference along with Showalter and Tommy, but all of the questions were about Browning's ejection, not the game-winning home run.

"Tommy, can you explain what hand lotion was doing in your glove?" someone asked.

"Dry hands," he replied with a slight sneer.

"You weren't trying to break the rules?"

"No, sir."

"Were you aware of the rules about foreign substances in or on your glove?"

"Yes, and that's all I'm going to say about it."

"What was your view of the ejection, Whitey? Has Tommy been doctoring the ball?"

The manager squirmed a little before answering. "He had hand lotion on his glove hand. Since when is it a crime to have dry skin?"

"In the summer?"

"It's possible. You get blisters and calluses from pitching all the time."

"But that wasn't his pitching hand," a questioner noted.

Showalter glared at the reporter and didn't respond at first. Then he fired back. "If the lotion was found in his glove and not on his pitching hand, what does it matter?"

The reporters grew silent while they attempted to understand that logic. Then they turned to Bagley for his take on the matter.

"What do you think, Hal? Does Browning do something illegal to the ball to get that crazy movement?"

Bagley cleared his throat and spoke slowly. "Tommy Browning throws a baseball like no human being I've ever seen. I don't care if you're using an emery board, sandpaper, grease, glue, or WD-40, you can't make a baseball move like that. He has a gift for pitching."

The reporters were quiet for a few seconds. They were either busy writing down Bagley's quote or checking their tape recorders to make sure they had it.

Finally, someone broke the silence. "Whitey, is Browning facing a suspension along with the ejection?"

"We haven't heard from the league office yet. I know they're doing a crackdown on so-called 'illicit grip aids,' so we'll just have to see what happens."

"Is that fair?"

"I don't think so." Showalter got up to leave the press conference, pushing his folding chair hard into the table.

After Tommy and the manager left the room, reporters soon followed, rushing to file their stories.

Bagley tried to stem the exodus and lighten the mood. "Anyone want to know about my home run? Anybody?"

CHAPTER 18

The next day, Tommy was notified that the commissioner's office was suspending him for two playoff games. However, that penalty grew lighter a few days later when the Braves beat the Brewers 5–4 in Milwaukee for a three-game sweep. Tommy wouldn't have opened the Series against the Dodgers-Giants winner anyway. Ty Barnwell was still the ace of the Braves staff, and a strong Cy Young Award candidate.

While Whitey Showalter and Hal Bagley publicly defended Tommy and believed the ejection and subsequent suspension were unwarranted, some players on the Braves began to wonder. Whispers of impropriety began to circulate throughout the clubhouse. Some teammates wondered if their phenom was cheating all along.

Ty revealed the gossip to Tommy, who was oblivious to the chatter going on behind his back.

"Dude, someone started a rumor about you in the clubhouse," he said after pulling Tommy aside. "Watch out, someone's out to get you."

"What do you mean? What kind of rumor?"

"They're saying you cheat. You're doing something illegal with the ball, using lotion on it or something. Some guys think you're on designer performance-enhancing drugs."

Tommy looked away in disgust. "My own teammates don't believe in me?"

"I do, man. I got your back. But you've got to stop those rumors for the good of the team."

"What can I do?" Tommy blurted back. "You'd think they'd be rooting for me, not back-stabbing me."

"First thing you've got to do is find out who started the rumor and confront him about it," Ty replied. "Do you have any idea who that is?"

Tommy thought long and hard before answering. "I think I know who the rat is," he said, frowning before turning away. "I'll deal with him."

When Tommy found Patrick Walker in the clubhouse, minutes after talking with Barnwell, the conversation immediately turned ugly. Other players heard their raised voices and backed away.

"You got something to say to me, Walker?" Tommy said. "Wanna say it to my face like a man?"

Walker looked surprised at first but his fangs soon came out. "Okay, I think you've been cheating all along. You're a fraud and we'll see that in the end." He poked his finger in Tommy's chest as he spoke.

"You're just out to get me," Tommy fired back. "You've been cold to me from the day I got here."

"You may be the media darling, but you ain't proved nothing to me yet, 'Browning Rifle,'" Walker said, pronouncing Tommy's nickname sarcastically. "I've been here for five years. I made the All-Star team this year. I've got twenty-six saves. You're just a fraud waiting to be exposed."

Tommy felt disrespected. Walker wouldn't even acknowledge his valuable contributions to the team, which included a near no-hitter and a team-best 1.68 ERA.

Instead, Walker continued on the offensive. "You won't be

around long, I'll bet on it. You're doing *something* illegal and you know it."

"No I'm not," Tommy shot back. "I've just got a great pitch."

"Well, if you're not doing something illegal, show me how you throw it. Show me your grip."

"I'm not going to do that."

"Show me your grip!" Walker repeated.

Tommy got silent.

"Just like I thought," Walker called out, as Tommy turned and walked away. Other players eyed the rookie suspiciously as he left the clubhouse.

CHAPTER 19

The two-game suspension ate away at Tommy like corrosive acid. He didn't think he was being treated fairly and couldn't wait to clear his name. That day would finally arrive when he took the mound to start Game 2 against the Dodgers in the National League Championship Series.

"I think he'll be fine," pitching coach Blasingame assured Showalter two days before the Series began. "He's on the road, away from home-crowd pressure, and he's pitching in a big ballpark against a team that hasn't seen him yet."

The Atlanta rotation seemed set, but the Dodgers threw a monkey wrench into the plans by beating Barnwell in the opener, 6–2. They knocked him out quickly with a five-run second inning.

"I want to make some pitching adjustments," Showalter said afterward. "We have to handle this Series differently now. I want to use four or five pitchers in Game 2 and concentrate on individual matchups. Just like how the Tampa Bay Rays do it. That might throw them off-balance."

Blasingame looked surprised. "Tommy could certainly throw them off-balance himself," he said.

"I know, but now we're placing some added pressure on a rookie . . . and one who just got thrown out of a game. I want to let him get his feet under him, maybe only go one time through the lineup. We've got the arms to play this way. I'm thinking we can bring Ty back two more times if the Series goes seven games. Maybe the same with Browning, if we limit his innings."

At first, the abrupt change in strategy sounded to Blasingame like Showalter was panicking. But the pitching coach went along with it. The Braves were blessed with a deep pitching staff. Why not use everyone?

When Tommy learned of the new strategy from Showalter, he wasn't happy, but he accepted the change. Rookies don't buck the manager—not even star rookies. He took the mound at Dodger Stadium feeling that once again he had something to prove. And there was no reason to pace himself.

The Tommy-Gun fastball exploded and, under the encouragement of Bagley, he increasingly worked in the new changeup to keep the Dodgers guessing. Tommy rarely shook off his catcher anymore when he put down three fingers.

"Don't be afraid of the change," Bagley said. "You're throwing it great."

"I'm going to let him go another inning or two," Showalter said to Blasingame after three scoreless innings, two scratch hits, and four strikeouts. "But that's it. We need to get the other guys involved and not let them see Browning too much. We'll need him later in the Series."

Tommy exited after five innings with a 2–0 lead and many of the Dodgers shaking their heads in disbelief. If the Braves held the lead, he was eligible for the win.

That looked promising in the ninth inning. By deftly mixing in two right-handers and a pair of lefties to control the pitching matchups, the Braves took the 2–0 lead into the bottom of the ninth and called on their closer, Walker. Walker gave up a bloop single to the leadoff batter but retired the Dodgers in order after that.

In the post-game celebration, Tommy was bestowed with most of the credit for evening the Series at a game apiece. Carlos

Lagares even gave him a hug. "You came up big for us, rook," he whispered in Tommy's ear. "I believe in you."

<hr/>

The Series shifted to Atlanta for three games with the Braves gaining confidence following the LA split. Showalter continued to juggle his mound staff while letting ace Barnwell and No. 3 starter John Anderson go midway into the game, similar to the way he'd used Tommy. Then he played mix-and-match with the bullpen.

That strategy worked like a charm. Barnwell bounced back after his rocky two innings in LA to pitch six scoreless innings. Anderson was impressive too, allowing one run over five. Up three games to one, the Braves were tantalizingly close to winning the best-of-seven Series.

Frustrated, the Dodgers demanded that Tommy's glove be checked for foreign substances during the third inning of Game 5, but there was nothing to find. Tommy was removed from the game with a comfortable 6–1 lead in the sixth and received a standing ovation.

The Dodgers didn't surrender. They closed to 6–5 with a sudden home run barrage, and the Braves tried desperately to hold on. No one wanted the Series to go back to the West Coast.

"Just one more out," Showalter said to himself in the ninth, nervously tapping his foot on the dugout steps. "C'mon, Patrick, put him away."

Walker went into his windup and threw a knee-buckling slider on the outside corner. Strike three!

The Atlanta Braves were headed back to the World Series.

CHAPTER 20

At 4:00 p.m. the next day, two local stars of sports talk radio hit the airwaves, eager to engage their loyal drive-time audience.

"Hello, Atlanta! Fritz and the Badger here with you on Sports Radio 620. What a beautiful Monday morning in A-town. How 'bout those Bra-a-a-a-ves!"

Fritz continued with his trademark high-pitched voice. "For the next three hours we'll be taking your calls and discussing the Braves, who are headed to the World Series for the second time in the twenty-first century. An amazing week for Atlanta sports, Badger."

"Couldn't be more excited, Fritzee."

"Before we take your calls, we're going to give a history lesson to put this moment in perspective. The Badger and I will review the pro-sports history in this city to, shall we say, fire up our audience. But we all know it. Aside from baseball, Atlanta has had a well-documented history of sports losers."

"No question about it, Fritz. Thank God we have the Braves."

"Let's start with the Falcons. They, of course, have never won a Super Bowl, and the 2017 Super Bowl loss to the Patriots is the nightmare of all sports nightmares. That collapse will never be forgotten. Leading 28–3 in the third quarter, we fell apart and lost 34–28 in overtime. That game was horrific. I don't care if we did lose to the greatest quarterback of all time, Tom Brady."

"A classic example of how not to sit on a lead, Fritz."

"But at least the Falcons *got* there," Fritz continued. The Hawks have never played for an NBA title since arriving in

Atlanta. That was more than half a century ago! The last time the Hawks won an NBA championship was in 1958 when they were in St. Louis."

"Yeah, and to give you an idea of how long ago that was, the 1958 St. Louis Hawks were the last team to win an NBA championship without a Black player on their roster." Badger chuckled after revealing the little-known piece of basketball trivia.

"Incredible, isn't it, Badger? They had a 6–9 center who dominated in Bob Pettit. He was a giant for the time.

"Should we look at hockey, too?" Fritz continued. "Well, there's not much to look at. Atlanta has had two NHL franchises, the Thrashers and the Flames. Both left for Canada. And hockey never came back.

"All right, now we get to the Braves. The Braves are the exception to the rule. They won the World Series over the Astros in 2021, taking the clinching game in Houston, 7–0. And now they're back again. They've had their share of success, wouldn't you say, Badger?"

"I wholeheartedly agree. Before they won the championship in 2021, you go back in history and they made World Series appearances in 1991, 1992, 1995, 1996, and 1999."

"The trouble is, they only won one World Series during that time—in 1995. And those teams had Hall of Famers John Smoltz, Greg Maddux, Tom Glavine, and Chipper Jones, plus Hall of Fame manager Bobby Cox."

"Definite underachievers, Fritz. But they kept running into the Yankees, who won four World-Series titles in five years."

"More recently, Badger, remember how the Braves lost the deciding Game 5 of the 2019 NLDS? The Cardinals scored ten runs in the first inning before the Braves *even came to bat*. They lost that game 13–1. It was a meltdown right from the opening pitch."

"Unbelievable, Fritzee. But the Braves redeemed themselves in 2021 and now we're back in the Series again. Hallelujah!"

"Badger, we should point out that the 2021 team was an underdog too, just like the Braves are this year. Maybe that's a good sign. Okay, let's open up the phone lines. I'm sure there are lots of people out there who want to talk Braves. Cecil from Roswell, you're on Sports Blitz."

"Hi, first-time caller, longtime listener. What do you think the Braves' chances are of beating the Yankees in the Series?"

"Make no mistake about it, the Yanks have an awesome club. They won 106 games this season and have home-run power to spare. It will be tough, but the Braves are peaking at the right time."

"Any predictions?" asked the caller.

"Not yet. Badger and I will give our predictions on tomorrow's show. Steven from Decatur, you're on the Blitz."

"Yes, I think that Tommy Browning is now the ace of the staff and should start the opener. What do you think?"

"Browning has been awesome, no doubt about it. He's good enough to start Game 1, even though he's a rookie. But that would mess up the rotation, and Ty Barnwell certainly deserves to start against the Yankees on the road. He'd probably fare better in the pressure cooker that's Yankee Stadium. What are your thoughts, Badger?"

"I agree. Start Barnwell in Game 1 on the road."

"Okay, now that we agree on that, here's Archie from Athens."

"How 'bout them Dawgs!"

"No, we're not talking Georgia football today, Archie. It's all Braves. Skeeter from Macon. What's up, Skeeter?"

"Daggumit, I was on hold so long I thought I'd lost y'all. I want to point out that all the coaches who worked with these Braves pitchers in the minor leagues deserve credit for developing them."

"Goes without saying, Skeeter. Anything else?"

"No, that's all I got."

"Fair enough. Here's Latrelle from East Point. What's happening, Latrelle?"

"Just chillin', man. Hey, I think this is a magical season like 2021. The way Browning pitches, there's magic in that man's arm. We're going all the way."

"Sure seems that way sometimes, Latrelle. Thanks for the call. One more before we go to the break, Badger. We've got another caller from Macon, a female this time. Ellie, what's on your mind?"

"I heard another caller talk about Tommy Browning starting Game 1. I don't think he can be trusted."

"Why would you say that, Ellie?"

"He doesn't have any sense of commitment. He's a snake."

"Okay . . . well, on that bizarre note, we've got to take our commercial break. We'll be back for more of your calls. You're listening to Sports Blitz with Fritz and the Badger on Sports Radio 620. Keep it here."

CHAPTER 21

Tommy sat in the Braves' dugout at Yankee Stadium, charting pitches. As the World-Series opening game unraveled, he felt the weight on his shoulders grow by the minute.

The Bronx Bombers had knocked out Ty Barnwell in the fifth, slamming back-to-back homers. That made it 4–1, and the Braves couldn't get much going against Soshi Igawa, the coveted Japanese pitcher the Yankees signed following a bidding war with the Angels, Red Sox, and the Dodgers.

The Yankees became a meat-grinder as the game wore on, chewing up Braves pitching. Four Atlanta pitchers gave up twelve total hits in an ugly 8–2 loss.

Afterward, the media reminded Showalter that he had a rookie going in Game 2, insinuating that one who started the year in Single-A would crumble before a raucous New York crowd.

"I have full confidence in Tommy Browning," the manager shot back. "He's not your ordinary rookie."

But Tommy had butterflies in his stomach as he prepared to take the mound the next night. He couldn't help but be nervous pitching for the first time in Yankee Stadium, starting a World-Series game with his team down 1–0 in the Series.

Before Tommy left the bullpen for the anxious walk out to the mound, Blasingame draped his arm around him. "Don't hold back, buddy. We're just looking for you to get through their lineup a couple of times, then we've got other guys rested. And use your changeup. You'll need it against their lineup."

Tommy nodded and hustled out to take care of business.

It soon became clear to Hal Bagley that Tommy wanted to rely on his Tommy-Gun pitch when he shook off several signals for a curve or changeup. And in fact, his one-of-a-kind fastball did have the Yankees off-balance, but that came after the No. 3 hitter jumped on a hanging curveball to go yard in the bottom of the first, giving New York a 1–0 lead.

The Braves got their bats going too. They bunched three hits and a walk in the third inning, staking Tommy to a 2–1 lead that he never relinquished. When Showalter pulled him after five innings, Browning's impressive pitching line read: one earned run, one home run, three hits, two walks, seven strikeouts.

"They're late on his fastball, and the Yankees devour fastball pitchers," Showalter marveled in the dugout. He prayed that he was making the right decision in pulling the spectacular rookie and placing the game in the hands of the bullpen.

A few anxious moments ticked by. The Yankees got two men on in the seventh and a runner reached third base in the ninth, but none of them scored. The Braves escaped New York with a 2–1 victory. The Series was now tied at a game apiece.

"I'll tell you, we're happy to be going back to Atlanta with a split," Showalter said to the media. "Lagares and Soto got key hits, and that guy over there was his usual amazing self."

Tommy heard the comment and smiled. He was now the winning pitcher in a World-Series game. Who would have believed that possible just three months ago?

CHAPTER 22

The Yankees came back strong to beat Anderson, 6–4, in Game 3, slugging three home runs. But Barnwell looked like his old self again in Game 4, allowing six hits and one run over six innings before the bullpen held on for a 3–2 Braves victory. The World Series was tied 2–2, heading into a pivotal Game 5. With the 2–3–2 format, the final two games were to be played in New York.

Ken Allen and Freddy Feld overlooked Atlanta's packed Truist Park from their broadcast booth.

Allen: "What a pitching matchup we have for our viewers tonight, the Yankees' Soshi Igawa versus the Browning Rifle, Tommy Browning, for the Braves. Freddy, you can't get a better matchup than that."

Feld: "You ain't just whistling Dixie, Ken. Soshi Igawa won nineteen games during the regular season, and Tommy Browning continues to surprise us every time he takes the bump."

Allen: "What are the keys for both teams tonight, Freddy?"

Feld: "For the Yankees, they need to clean up their defense a little. They've made a few sloppy errors in the field—both mental and physical—that have to be eliminated. They've thrown to the wrong base, had some passed balls, and failed to keep runners close. Of course, when you hit home runs like they do, that covers up for a lot of sins."

Allen: "And for the Braves?"

Feld: "Browning needs to get ahead of the hitters like he did in Game 2 in New York. When pitchers get behind in the count, Yankees hitters really tee off. Also, they need to get Carlos Lagares on base and let him run. He stole thirty bases during the season and puts a heckuva lot of pressure on a defense."

Allen: "One thing is clear. The Braves need this game at home so they don't have to take two straight in New York. That would be asking a lot."

Feld: "They've sure got this crowd behind them. Atlanta fans are pumped for another title."

Allen: "Yankees versus Braves, Game 5. Back in a minute."

First Inning

Allen: "Strike three called! Tommy Browning opens the game by striking out the side. Braves coming to bat."

Fifth Inning

Allen: "Browning has now struck out ten Yankees in this scoreless game. He also has not allowed a baserunner."

Feld: "He's got the Bronx Bombers swinging at air, all right. They're behind on his fastball and way out in front of his changeup. He's mixing that in deftly. He hasn't thrown many curveballs, but when he has, they've had bite."

Allen: "But Igawa has only allowed two hits, and no Brave has reached second base."

Seventh Inning

Allen: "We're still scoreless heading to the bottom of the seventh. Braves pitcher Tommy Browning has not allowed a baserunner. If the Braves can scratch out a run, we may be watching history in the making."

Feld: "Let's not jinx him. He's already lost a no-hitter in the eighth."

Allen: "But I have to say, this is the sharpest we've ever seen Browning—and that's saying something."

Feld: "Well, the Yankees have to change their approach at the plate. They're a home-run-hitting team, and many of them have long, looping swings. You can't do that against a fastball that explodes like Browning's. They need to cut down on their swings and concentrate on making contact.

"The problem is, major-league hitters never want to change their swings for a particular pitcher. That's why they hate facing knuckleballers."

Allen: "And that's a tough adjustment for a team that gets nearly 60 percent of its runs from the long ball."

Feld: "You can't turn a porcupine into an otter."

Allen: "What's that supposed to mean?"

Feld: "You know, a porcupine has quills. It will never be an otter. Otters swim. Different animal. Different skills."

Allen: "Okay . . . that's, uh, quite an analogy, Freddy."

Eighth Inning

Allen: "For any viewers who are just tuning in, we've got a scoreless Game 5 between the Yankees and the Braves, and Atlanta pitcher Tommy Browning has not allowed a baserunner yet. As we head to the bottom of the eighth, the Braves have eight, nine, and one coming up in their order to face Soshi Igawa. That's Higueras, Browning, and Chang.

"Caesar Higueras steps in against Igawa. He jumps on the first pitch and lines a base hit to left field. The Braves have a baserunner. Only the fourth hit off Igawa. Now it gets interesting, Freddy. Do you pinch-hit for a guy who's pitching a perfect game?"

Feld: "That's the difficult decision Whitey Showalter will have to make."

Allen: "Browning has been up just nine times in his major-league career. He does not have a hit. He's struck out in both plate appearances tonight."

Feld: "He's no Tony Cloninger. Cloninger was a pitcher for the Braves who hit two grand slams in a game in 1966, the first year the team was in Atlanta after the move from Milwaukee."

Allen: "One of the best-hitting pitchers of all time. Of course, the greatest was Babe Ruth, with all due respect to Shohei Ohtani."

Feld: "Browning is being called back from the on-deck circle, and here come the boos."

Allen: "Wait, he's meeting with Whitey. Do you think they're just telling him to bunt?"

Feld: "Probably. Here he comes, and the crowd's giving him a standing ovation."

Allen: "Browning steps in against Igawa. Takes high, ball one."

Feld: "He's showing bunt."

Allen: "High again, ball two."

Feld: "You just have to throw a strike here."

Allen: "Igawa delivers on 2–0. Browning tries to bunt and fouls it off."

Feld: "Well, he got a piece of it."

Allen: "The next pitch is low and outside. It's 3–1. Igawa's in danger of walking the pitcher. Do you think they give Browning the 'take' sign or try to bunt again?"

Feld: "I would give him the take."

Allen: "Bunted foul. Full count."

Feld: "Now I wouldn't have him bunt, but I would have him just take a pitch and hope Igawa misses again."

Allen: "Here's the windup. Browning swings and hits a soft-liner over first base. It drops! Higueras will go all the way to third base."

Feld: "Browning couldn't have placed that any better. Right down the first baseline. He hit it right off the end of the bat."

Allen: "Browning is practically jumping for joy at first base. The Braves have runners on the corners with no outs. The Yankees pull their infield in. They're going to try to cut off Higueras at third."

Feld: "Chang pops up on the first pitch for an out. Now the Yanks may decide to play their infield back and go for a double play. If you're Igawa, you want to use your sinker and get a ground ball."

Allen: "Devin Nelson steps in. He takes a second sinker low. He's ahead of the count 2–0."

Feld: "If you're Nelson, look for something you can lift for a fly ball."

Allen: "Nelson hits a fly ball to center field. It's deep enough. Higueras tags and he'll score. The throw is cut and Browning remains at first base. The Braves lead 1–0."

Feld: "The throw home was cut off, but Browning had no intentions of going to second. That would have been suicide."

Top of the Ninth Inning

Allen: "Tommy Browning is three outs away from baseball immortality. In 1956, Don Larsen of the Yankees pitched the only perfect game in World-Series history with a 2–0 win over the Brooklyn Dodgers in Game 5. Browning has a chance to repeat that accomplishment tonight in Game 5 against the Yankees."

Feld: "If he does, I wonder if Hal Bagley will jump into Browning's arms like Yogi Berra did with Larsen."

Allen: "The count is 1–2 on O'Toole. Strike three swinging! Browning now has sixteen strikeouts and is two outs away from perfection.

"Number three hitter Tevan Reynolds is up. He swings at the first pitch and hits a deep drive to center field. Lagares goes back to the edge of the warning track. He makes the catch!"

Feld: "That was the longest ball we've seen hit off Tommy tonight."

Allen: "Browning is now one out away from a perfect game and putting his club up three games to two. Fans are making their way down to the box seats. They may storm the field if he gets this out. But Yankees slugger Stephan Baker is stepping to the plate.

"Baker takes ball two high. Browning has been ahead most of the night, but the count runs to 2–0. And there's ball three, just off the inside corner."

Feld: "That just missed. Now he has to throw a strike."

Allen: "Swing and a miss. Baker was swinging on 3–0."

Feld: "Not what I would have done, but that shows the confidence the Yankees have in a guy who walloped forty-seven homers during the regular season."

Allen: "Fouled off. Baker had a good rip at a fastball but fouled it straight back. Full count. Baseball immortality is on the line."

Feld: "The fans look ready to pounce."

Allen: "Browning delivers. Hit hard . . . caught by Soto! Perfect game! Perfect game! Third baseman Javier Soto dove to his left and stabbed a vicious line drive to end the game. Braves win, 1–0."

Feld: "And Browning gave him a huge fist pump. Here come the fans! They're storming the field."

Allen: "And Tommy is sprinting to the dugout, picking his way through the crowd."

Feld: "What a way to go out! This was the last home game for the Braves regardless of what happened, and the fans are going wild. History is made!"

When the players were safely in the clubhouse, Tommy rushed over to Soto and gave him a bear hug. "Great play. You saved me tonight, man."

Soto just nodded and smiled back.

One by one, back safely in the clubhouse, players filed by Tommy to offer their congratulations.

Whitey Showalter gave him a hug too. "Greatest World-Series performance I've ever seen," he whispered. "Don't worry that you couldn't get the bunt down. We'll work on that in practice." He playfully mussed up Tommy's hair.

Seconds later the Braves' public relations director whisked Tommy away to the media room to answer questions from the eager horde of writers and broadcasters.

Tommy couldn't feel his feet touch the ground. He felt like he was walking on air.

CHAPTER 23

The euphoria was quickly dashed two days later when the Yankees bounced back with a 5–2 win in New York, tying the Series at three games apiece.

A three-run homer by Baker—who had earned the nickname "Home-Run Baker" after a star who'd played for the Yankees from 1916–1922—was the crushing blow. Baker's blast was sweet revenge after being robbed by Soto in Game 5.

Showalter called an impromptu team meeting in the Braves' clubhouse before game seven. He moved to the center of the floor and surveyed his players.

"Listen up, fellas. I want everybody ready and available to play tonight. If you're hurt, let me know. This is do-or-die and it's all hands on deck—pardon my clichés. Position players, if you don't start be ready at a moment's notice to pinch-hit, pinch-run, or go in as a defensive replacement."

All eyes remained fixed on the manager. The clubhouse was silent except for Showalter's voice.

"Pitchers, I might call on you to get two batters or throw a couple of innings. It depends on the situation. Herb is going to be beside me in the dugout, and we'll take advantage of righty-lefty matchups. I'm sure they'll have their share of lefty sticks in the lineup trying to take advantage of that 314 sign down the rightfield line. So, be ready if we call on you. That's all."

The players clapped heartily as the manager turned and headed back to his office. The Braves appeared focused but loose for a World-Series Game 7. Music came back on and there was laughter.

Showalter abruptly stopped and turned around. He called out to Tommy and waved for him to come over. "Tommy, I know you've only had two days' rest after pitching nine innings in Atlanta. I'd love to have you available again, but I understand if you're too sore."

"I only threw 128 pitches. I can still go an inning or two," Tommy said.

Showalter returned an appreciative smile, "Well, all right, I'll see if we need you."

Game 7 stayed scoreless through seven innings as the Braves mixed and matched their pitchers against the Yankees. Anderson started and pitched his three best innings of the Series, followed by two good innings from Barnwell and brief stints from three Atlanta relievers. However, the Yankees left runners on in four different innings and looked like they might break through at any time.

The Braves also squandered base runners but stunned the New York crowd when Devin Nelson lined a double down the leftfield line, driving in Higueras and Chang in the eighth for a 2–0 Atlanta lead. That double landed like a smothering blanket, extinguishing the fire in the raucous Yankee fans.

A solo home run in the bottom of the eighth narrowed the score to 2–1 and reignited the New York crowd.

Showalter turned to his pitching coach, who was seated beside him. "Get Walker and Browning up," he said, urgency in his voice.

Braves lefthander Craig Miller was able to retire the first two hitters in the bottom of the ninth, but the noise level rose again when he walked the next batter on four pitches.

"If he doesn't get this next guy, I'm going to bring in Browning," Showalter said, leaning in toward Blasingame.

Blasingame looked surprised. "Not Patrick? He's our closer, and we've got the lead."

"I know, but Baker's on deck and I like that matchup, even though Baker hit a frozen rope against him last time," Showalter said. "And I'd rather save Walker for extra innings. I think Tommy's only good for a batter or two."

"C'mon, Craig, throw strikes!" Blasingame pleaded. But when the count reached 2–0, he called timeout and walked slowly to the mound to talk to his pitcher. The visit was mostly to stall for time.

"If this guy gets on, Browning's going in," Showalter repeated, as soon as Blasingame returned to the dugout. It was a risky, unconventional move, but Showalter was going with his gut. Plus, it was a righthanded-pitcher-versus-righthanded-batter matchup. Maybe Tommy could get Baker to chase curveballs off the outside of the plate or succumb to a fastball high and tight.

The next pitch was a strike, but it was drilled up the middle for a base hit. Runners on first and second, two outs.

Showalter went to the mound and took the ball from Miller's hand.

As Tommy nervously walked in from the bullpen, he realized he could go from World-Series hero to goat in the span of one bad pitch. His dream Series was on the line. He tried to stay confident. If he could just get Home-Run Baker out, he'd be the toast of Atlanta. They'd probably name a street after him and he'd never have to pick up a dinner check or bar tab again.

He felt some stiffness in warm-ups, but nothing major. Still, a little stiffness could have big consequences if it took a couple of miles per hour off his Tommy-Gun pitch. He recalled the pitch Baker had drilled the other night—a fastball. Good thing Soto speared the line drive.

Once again, Tommy fell behind in the count against Baker. But he wanted to be careful. A walk wouldn't be disastrous; it would load the bases, but he only needed one out. However, an extra base hit would end the Series.

Tommy recalled how Baker swung on a 3–0 count the last time he faced him. He was sitting on a fastball. With that in mind, Tommy surprised the Yankees star with a curveball on 2–0, and he took it for a strike.

Then, thinking Baker would be looking fastball again, he threw a changeup and caught the Yankees slugger well out in front of the ball for a swinging strike. Bagley signaled for a fastball at 2–2 and was insistent when Tommy tried to shake him off. Finally, the catcher called time and went to the mound.

"Throw the damn fastball! That's your best pitch," the catcher scolded.

"But he's a fastball hitter," Tommy said.

"I don't care," Bagley replied. "If you get beat, get beat with your best."

The umpire was about to head to the mound, so Tommy finally gave in. "I'll give you a target high and inside," Bagley said. "He has a hard time holding up on that pitch."

Tommy nodded. After all, if Baker took the pitch it would only be ball three. But, he reminded himself, if the pitch missed its location and sailed over the middle of the plate, his storybook season could end in a nightmare: a three-run homer.

Or the fastball could hit Baker if he dove into the pitch but didn't swing. That would load the bases.

He steadied himself, moved into the stretch position, and stayed there for what seemed like an excessively long time. The crowd tried to rattle him with ear-shattering noise.

But Tommy concentrated on the catcher's glove. Finally, he launched into his delivery.

The pitch was right where Bagley wanted it. It exploded into his glove as Baker took a ferocious cut and missed.

The dugout erupted in celebration. Showalter hugged Blasingame. Tommy threw his glove so high in the air it didn't seem like it would ever come down. The upstart Braves were World-Series champions!

In the next few seconds, Tommy found himself in an odd position: under a dogpile of adoring teammates.

Within minutes, he was unanimously named World Series Most Valuable Player.

CHAPTER 24

Two days after the Braves' charter flight returned to Atlanta, wrapped in glory, Tommy found himself back in New York City.

"Welcome to the *Tonight Show*," belted out the host, Jimmy Diamond. "We've got an incredible show for you tonight: World Series hero Tommy Browning and recording legend Beyoncé are here!"

Diamond soon launched into his monologue and stuck in a joke involving his male guest. "A man in Saginaw, Michigan, woke up twenty million dollars richer after finding the winning lottery ticket on the street. To which Tommy Browning said, 'Hey, you think you had a good year?'"

Immediately following the monologue, Tommy was called out for his show-business debut.

"My first guest is coming off a classic World-Series performance in which he pitched the Atlanta Braves to two wins— one a perfect game— and saved another game in relief. He even got a key hit to help them win. What, is that all?" Diamond deadpanned.

"The Braves beat the Yankees, four games to three, to win the World Series in an upset. I know we have Yankees fans in our audience," Diamond said with a cautious smile, "but please give a warm welcome to Tommy Browning."

Tommy came out to scattered boos. "All right, all right, sportsmanship," Diamond said, playfully admonishing the crowd.

"Yankees fans haven't forgiven you," Diamond said as

Tommy sat down next to the *Tonight Show* desk. "I saw a few doing the tomahawk chop, but I think they were aiming at your neck."

The joke brought howls from the audience.

"Seriously, it's a thrill to have you on the show. I'm going to read what one sportswriter from the *New York Times* wrote about you: 'Mr. Browning's sterling performance puts him up with Madison Bumgarner, Christy Mathewson, Bob Gibson, Randy Johnson, Don Larsen and Grover Cleveland Alexander in the pantheon of pitchers who have achieved World-Series immortality.'

"Not bad for a guy who started the baseball season in Single-A," Diamond added.

Tommy threw his hands up and smirked. He appeared comfortable being the center of attention. "Thank you, Jimmy. I don't know what to say. I feel like I'm living a dream."

"By August you made the huge leap to the major leagues. How was that possible?"

"Well, I developed a new pitch."

"The Tommy Gun," Jimmy quickly cut in.

"Right. Anyway, my fastball got a lot better."

"Okay, I happen to have a baseball right here," Diamond said, pulling out a ball from behind the desk. "Can you show our audience how you grip it?"

Tommy had been asked that so many times, mostly by fellow pitchers. He had a standard reply waiting for deflection. "If I told you that, Jimmy, I'd have to kill you." He smiled devilishly.

Diamond played along. "No, no, no, I worked too hard to get this job."

Tommy laughed. "I don't want to lose my job either," he said.

After some more banter, the host inquired about his guest's off-season plans.

"I'm just going to rest my arm and see what comes my way," Tommy said. "I'm sure I'll be busy."

"I bet our TV audience is dying to know, do you have a girlfriend?"

"I'm playing the field," Tommy said with a wink.

"Well, the *Tonight Show* wants you to enjoy an experience you missed out on in the excitement of the perfect game. When Don Larsen pitched his perfect game, catcher Yogi Berra ran out to the pitching mound and jumped into his arms. We have a lovely girl who would happily do the same thing for you in a reenactment of the scene. Would you like that?"

Tommy straightened up in his seat and leaned forward. "I'd love to," he said with a wide grin.

The two walked over to the stage, and Diamond handed Tommy a Wiffle ball. "Let's bring out Bessie, our catcher," he announced.

From behind the curtain, a chimpanzee hopped out, holding the hand of her trainer. The chimp was wearing baseball pajamas with the words "Atlanta Apes" across the front. She also wore a little baseball cap tied on her head with a string, like a birthday hat.

The trainer handed Bessie a plastic baseball glove. The chimp lowered into a crouching position.

"Okay, throw Bessie the ball, Tommy," Diamond said, hardly suppressing his laughter.

This was hardly the girl Tommy had expected, but he wanted to be a good sport and tossed the Wiffle ball underhand to the chimp. Bessie scooped it up, bounced over to Tommy, and jumped into his arms.

"Just like how Yogi did it!" Diamond announced.

The long arms of the chimp wrapped around Tommy's shoulders. She rested her head right next to his. The ape hugged hard. The audience roared in laughter.

Tommy's only thought was: *Why couldn't it have been Beyoncé?*

CHAPTER 25

When Tommy arrived back in Atlanta, he got a call from the general manager of the Braves.

"We want to write up a new contract for you, Tommy," Steve Bailey said.

Bailey had previously met with Showalter. They decided that in order to create goodwill and pave the way for re-signing their new superstar before he reached free agency, it would be best to act now. An unusual gesture toward someone who had only been in the big leagues a few months.

Tommy felt a rush of excitement. "Should I bring an agent?" he inquired.

Bailey hesitated for a few seconds. "Do you have an agent?"

"No, not right now," Tommy said.

"Well, you can find one if you don't want to represent yourself. Ask the other players. They can probably refer you to someone we've worked with."

When Tommy got off the phone, he immediately called Ty Barnwell, explained the situation, and asked him about his agent. "I'll give you his number, man," Barnwell said. "He'll take care of you for sure. He'll get you the green you deserve. His name is Kevin Shapiro. He doesn't monkey around, bro."

Tommy cringed at the joke while Barnwell cracked up laughing on the other end of the line.

"I saw you on the *Tonight Show*," Ty said. "It was funny, man."

"It was kind of embarrassing," Tommy said.

"Nah, it's all good. You got to meet Beyoncé, right?"

"Sure did. She came on after me and the chimp. She's gorgeous."

When he got off the phone with his teammate, Tommy called Shapiro, who was more than happy to take him on as a client. "I'll only charge you three percent commission," Shapiro offered. "Most agents want four or five."

"Should I be in the room with you during negotiations?" Tommy asked.

"No, let me handle it. I'll get you a good deal."

Two days later, Bailey and Shapiro got together behind closed doors in Bailey's office in Truist Park. Bailey seemed glad that Tommy chose Shapiro as his agent. He knew he could work with him. Shapiro was usually tough but realistic. Bailey was shocked when the agent came right out and asked for six years and three hundred million.

"You want to wrap him up long term, don't you? How much do you think he'll be worth heading into free agency after four full years?" Shapiro said.

Bailey shook his head in disbelief. "He's been in the big leagues for less than half a season, Kevin."

"But he's coming off the greatest World-Series performance ever," Shapiro said. "The Braves wouldn't have won the World Series—or even the National League pennant—without him."

"And we want to reward your client for it," Bailey replied. "But not that much."

"You've got a lot to lose if he skips town. Tommy Browning may be a transcendent talent."

"Or a flash in the pan," Bailey said. "Pitchers get hurt. You know that's why I don't like to give them long-term contracts, especially one as inexperienced as Tommy." He peered down at some numbers he'd written on a piece of paper. "I'm thinking no more than three years, preferably two," he said. "After three years he's eligible for arbitration."

Talks continued for most of the day while Tommy kept his phone near. Finally, around 4:30 in the afternoon, Shapiro exited Bailey's office and called Tommy.

"They didn't want to go long term," he reported, "and you can't go anywhere else for a while. I got you two years and forty-two, guaranteed. You okay with that?"

"Forty-two?" Tommy asked.

"Million."

Tommy dropped the phone and broke into his Money Dance. He was going to be rich.

CHAPTER 26

Tommy showed up with his agent in Bailey's office a few weeks later to go over terms of the whopping contract before signing it. He couldn't help but stare at the World-Series trophy sitting tall on a shelf behind the general manager.

Bailey looked over his shoulder to see what Tommy was fixated on. "Oh, the trophy is just on loan in my office," he said almost apologetically. "The team owner wants everyone to get some time with it before he parks it in his office."

The sterling-silver Commissioner's Trophy featured gold-plated flags for each major-league team. It seemed surreal to see it residing with the Braves.

"You both have a copy of the contract in front of you. Follow along while I read it to you," Bailey said.

He stopped for emphasis after going over a clause about "assuming unreasonable risks" that could legally void the contract.

"That means no basketball, no skydiving, motorcycling, skiing, snowboarding or skateboarding, hang gliding, bungee jumping or off-roading on ATVs. And don't start throwing the javelin thinking you're going to make the US Olympic team," Bailey said with a laugh.

"No basketball?" Tommy asked.

"Nope. We can't have you tearing an ACL in the off-season. Your body belongs to us."

Tommy nodded. Even though he loved to play basketball, he wasn't about to argue. "What about golf?"

"It probably wouldn't void your contract, but don't play eighteen holes on days that you're pitching," Bailey said. "That's common sense."

Bailey handed Tommy a pen to sign on the dotted line. Tommy's hand shook with excitement. With one stroke of a pen, he was about to change his life forever.

"Oh, and by the way, you'll be getting a full World Series share on top of this," Bailey said. "That's $395,000 from the player pool."

The ink on his contract was barely dry before Tommy began to plan his dream home. He couldn't wait to build in Newnan, his hometown.

Tommy found five wooded acres for sale on the outskirts of Newnan. The land included a large lake, and deer roamed freely throughout the property. The lake was so pretty and the land so pristine, he couldn't pass it up.

He met with several builders in Coweta County, going over proposals and blueprints before settling on a contractor. This would be his dream house: eight thousand square feet, stone exterior, five bedrooms, six baths, hardwood floors, an entertainment center, and pool. The price tag: $3 million.

Thanks to the huge contract he signed with the Braves, he could easily afford it. He secured a mortgage within weeks.

The future looked even brighter after Kevin Shapiro called Tommy one Tuesday in the off-season.

"Dude, my phone's been ringing constantly since we hooked up," the agent said. "I'm getting proposals for you every day."

"From women?" Tommy asked, confused.

"No, from businesses. They want you to be their spokesman

and endorse their products. You might say they want you as their 'pitch man.'"

"Really? What do I have to do?"

"No heavy lifting. Maybe appear in a print ad or in a commercial," Shapiro said. "Sometimes it's just to allow them to say you use a sports cream or something."

"No kidding? How many offers have we gotten?"

"At least a dozen and they keep coming in."

"I'll endorse as many things as I can," Tommy said, seeing dollar signs in his head.

"Not so fast," Shapiro cautioned. "We've got to be selective. You don't want to be overexposed. That can hurt your marketability. On the other hand," Shapiro added following a short pause, "it's best to strike while the iron's hot."

"Which offers should we take?" Tommy asked.

"Let me run two by you. First, how do you feel about Chick-fil-A? As I'm sure you know, it's a Georgia company and a very successful fast-food chain. They're everywhere in this state and growing nationwide."

Tommy didn't hesitate. "I love 'em! I always eat their spicy chicken sandwiches."

"Okay, great. We can probably get big money out of them."

"I'm one-hundred-percent on board," Tommy said.

"The other offer I had in mind is a bigger commitment, but should bring greater reward," Shapiro said. "Browning Arms Company wants Tommy Browning as its spokesman. You're not related to them, are you?"

"No, but I could do it. I've hunted deer with a rifle since I was fourteen. And I've shot Browning rifles."

"Seems like a natural fit," Shapiro said. "They make quality firearms, and fans already call you the Browning Rifle. Browning may pay millions."

"Let's go for it," Tommy said without a moment's hesitation.

"Okay, I'll get back to you," Shapiro said and hung up.

By February, Tommy had signed lucrative endorsement deals with Coca-Cola, Chick-fil-A, Sunglass Hut, Hooters, Russell Sportswear—and Browning.

The money was flowing like honey.

CHAPTER 27

One crisp morning in Fayetteville, Tommy strode confidently onto an outdoor film set wearing green camouflage, a hunter's orange vest, and a Browning baseball cap. He was about to shoot his first television commercial, and he was visibly excited.

"Do I get to shoot the rifle or just hold it?" he asked the director.

"You can fire it at that target over there," the director replied, pointing to a circular target with colorful rings set up about thirty feet away in an open field. "I want you to look comfortable, like you've shot a Browning rifle before."

"Oh, I have," Tommy said.

"You don't have to get a bull's-eye," the director quickly added. "We don't care about accuracy. Just shoot in that direction and have a satisfied look on your face. Then hold the rifle in front of the camera and say your lines."

"Can I take the rifle home?"

"We'll send you a brand-new one as part of the deal. You have a gun license, don't you?"

"You don't really need one to get a gun in Georgia," Tommy replied.

"Really? Gun laws are pretty loose down here," the director said.

"It's legal to carry a concealed handgun," Tommy pointed out, "and I've never needed a license for my hunting rifle."

Shapiro jumped into the conversation from the sidelines. "You sure you have your lines down, Tommy?" he asked.

"Yeah, I got this."

"Okay," said the director. "Let's go."

With cameras rolling, Tommy aimed and fired his gun at the circular target. Then he stared straight into the camera.

"Hi, I'm Tommy Browning of the Atlanta Braves," he said, dropping the rifle from his shoulder. "They call me the Browning Rifle, which is a high compliment, because there's no better firearm than a Browning. It's what I use for hunting game, and you should too."

Tommy went on to read some specs and model names off cue cards before closing his endorsement. "Browning firearms: they're the guns for champions."

"Cut. Very good!" the director shouted, visibly pleased. "Let's roll it back. We may not even have to do another take."

Tommy rushed over to look at his target—his shot was a near bull's-eye.

"Nice job, dude," Shapiro said, extending his hand to Tommy. "You just opened the door for more TV spots."

"What else do I have to do for the Browning Company?" he asked.

"I think they plan to run some print and online ads with your image, plus a few personal appearances," Shapiro answered. "Nothing too heavy, considering they're paying you three million dollars."

Tommy looked up to the heavens. "That will pay for my new house."

"Hey, Tommy," Shapiro said, ushering him closer. "You're scoring big with me, but let's keep it between ourselves that I'm only charging you 3 percent commission. Ty and some of my other athletes might get jealous."

Tommy smiled back. "No problem, Kevin. I can keep a

secret." He turned to the director. "When do you think I'll get my rifle?"

"In a week or two. I'll get it expedited."

Tommy rubbed his hands together, a completely satisfied man. At that moment he considered putting a bumper sticker on his BMW: *Life is good.*

CHAPTER 28

While Tommy was raking in cash, the Braves' public relations director, Lexie Doolittle, was practically tearing out her hair.

"What will it take to get you to make some personal appearances for the Braves?" she asked Tommy one afternoon on a phone call. "You're our hottest player. Why won't you agree to speak to some civic organizations?"

Tommy, reclining on a sofa in his Buckhead apartment, sat up a bit. "I'm just too busy right now, Lexie."

"But it's the off-season," she replied.

"I know, but I got my house going up, and I'm looking around to buy a yacht to keep down in Florida."

"Tommy, these fundraisers are for good causes. You've given me every excuse in the book, and frankly, some are pretty ridiculous."

Tommy went on defense. "Which ones?" he asked.

"You wouldn't speak to the Veterans of Foreign Wars because you say you're against war. You don't want any connection with Habitat for Humanity in case one of their houses collapses. You say you won't support Feed the Children because that's what their parents are for. And," she added, sounding totally exasperated, "you refused the Shriners because you don't like their hats or the little motor bikes they ride on in parades."

"Yeah, it makes them look silly," Tommy said. "That's not the image my agent wants me to project."

Lexie shook her head before speaking again. "Come on, this

is really about money, isn't it? You won't do it because you're not getting paid."

"Why should I? My time is valuable. And, I don't want to cheapen my brand by speaking for free."

"The civic groups we support are the lifeblood of our Atlanta community," Lexie said. "Don't you want to help?"

There was silence on the other end of the line.

"Hello? Tommy?"

Tommy sounded more belligerent. "Like I said, I'm busy."

"You can't even do one appearance?"

"Not now," Tommy said. "And I wish you'd stop calling me."

"Well, please let me know if you change your mind." Lexie abruptly ended the call.

Tommy went back to rereading a magazine story written about him—for the third time.

"Who was that on the phone?" came a female voice from the kitchen.

"No one, babe," Tommy said, pulling his laptop computer in closer.

"You want another frozen margarita?"

"Sure, keep 'em coming, and bring me more of those big shrimp too," Tommy said, looking up. "Hey, what did you say your name was again?"

CHAPTER 29

February 18 snuck up on Tommy with the same stealth as his Tommy-Gun pitch confronted batters. That was the day Braves pitchers and catchers reported to spring training.

Between serving as product pitchman and overseeing the construction of his dream house, the off-season had flown by. Time to go back to work. But Tommy never thought of his baseball career as work, even during those trying times in Single-A. Ever since the day he played catch for the first time, he considered baseball a fanciful game, one that he simply loved to play.

As he drove his BMW to CoolToday Park, the ninety-acre facility in North Port, Florida where the Braves conducted spring training, he couldn't wait to see his teammates and be welcomed back as the conquering hero.

But as soon as he approached the gate, he spotted a commotion. There were a dozen or more protesters outside holding signs and marching around while chanting. Tommy squinted to read some of the signs.

"More guns = more deaths!"

"Browning's words kill!"

"Put a silencer on the Browning Rifle!"

Tommy didn't drive any closer. But before he could figure out an escape plan, one of the protesters cried out, "There he is!" Within seconds his car was surrounded by an angry mob. A television crew rushed over to film the confrontation.

"There were 158 homicides in the city of Atlanta last year,

the most in more than two decades. Most of those were gun related. Shame on you for promoting guns," came an agitated voice from outside his car.

The TV newswoman tapped on Tommy's driver-side window, urging him to roll it down and respond. Tommy sighed and reluctantly complied. She shoved her microphone inside the car as the camera rolled. The mic hit Tommy in the face.

"I've never shot anyone," he said defensively. "I only use guns to hunt deer."

That didn't appease the protesters. "Don't promote guns! Don't promote guns!" they chanted. To Tommy, the gathering looked more like a lynch mob than a peaceful protest.

The newswoman moved her mic back in front of a protester. "We need gun control. It's common sense!" the person commented.

"I gotta go," Tommy said, quickly closing his power window. He crept his car forward, parting the crowd while taking care not to make contact with anyone. *If I hit someone, I'll be sued*, he thought.

Once he made it to the gate a security man checked for identification. "Nice to meet you, Tommy. Great World Series." His welcoming smile was reassuring, a security blanket of sorts, and more like what Tommy expected.

"Hey, you look a little rattled," the man said. "Don't worry. That's public property out there, but they can't enter the facility."

Tommy sighed in relief as the security man opened the gate.

"Go Braves!" the man yelled from behind as Tommy drove his car through.

When he entered the clubhouse, players rushed up to greet Tommy and welcome him back. His teammates were warm and inviting. He didn't detect any ill will for the generous new contract he'd signed, although nearly all of the players were aware of it. Kenny Battle, a middle reliever who went to Princeton and fancied himself an investment guru, was short and sweet.

"One word: cryptocurrency," Battle said.

Tommy entered Whitey Showalter's office to check in. "Hey, welcome back, pardner," the manager said, rising from his chair to shake his star's hand. "Bet you didn't expect *that* reception outside."

"How long have they been there?" Tommy asked.

"Since early this morning. But I bet they'll be gone soon. Don't give it another thought."

Tommy smiled weakly.

"Hey, I hardly recognized you with the short hair."

"Chick-fil-A wanted me to cut it for their ads, so I said okay," Tommy said.

"Ready for a repeat?" Showalter said. "It'll be tougher now that we're the champs. Everybody's trying to knock us off."

"I'm all in, Skip," Tommy replied.

"Thatta boy. It sure would be sweet to repeat." The manager grinned. "Bet you didn't know I was a poet, did you?"

The first day of spring training consisted of stretching, some light throwing, and meeting with pitching coach Blasingame. It seemed like more of a social event than hard work.

"We've got you behind Ty as number two in our rotation this season, Tommy," Blasingame said. "That's a pretty good combo to start: last year's Cy Young runner-up, and the World-Series MVP."

Tommy was pumped. "Maybe we can both win twenty games," he suggested. "I know I can."

"That's a goal to shoot for," Blasingame said. "But it's tough nowadays. Starting pitchers don't throw complete games anymore. Hell, five or six innings is considered a quality start."

"Maybe I'll change all that," Tommy said confidently. "I can go nine."

"I like your attitude, but it's my job to protect your arm," Blasingame said.

When practice ended, Tommy guardedly left the facility to check in at the Hampton Inn, an extended-stay hotel where he planned to reside during spring training. The coast was clear—no protesters.

In five more days, the position players would report. Then the fun would really begin.

CHAPTER 30

The next day Tommy arrived at CoolToday Park and almost choked on the breakfast burrito he was stuffing in his mouth.

The protesters were back. This time they carried different signs:

"Be a dear, shoot Browning!"

"Bambi says Tommy sucks!"

"Deer lives matter!"

Tommy shook his head. *I thought they'd be gone.*

He quickly plotted his strategy, waiting for another car to arrive for cover. Luckily, someone drove up in a Nissan Armada. Tommy made his move, following close behind in the giant SUV's shadow. He plowed ahead, ducking his body under the dashboard of his car with his eyes barely above it.

He peeked into his rearview mirror. Someone with antlers on their head suddenly recognized the white BMW. "There's Browning!" he yelled, and the protesters rushed toward him in a tidal wave.

"Hurry up," Tommy prodded the Armada. He was about to hit his horn when his cover vehicle accelerated through the gate. The security man saw the angry crowd advancing and waved the Armada through, Tommy's BMW hot on its heels.

When Tommy was safely inside the complex, he marched straight into Showalter's office. "I thought you told me they'd be gone by today," he said.

"They are," Showalter replied. "The anti-gun folks *are* gone. Now the PETA people are here."

Tommy shot off to the safety of the clubhouse, and then the baseball field. He ran into Ty Barnwell, who was reporting to camp a day late after dealing with a personal issue.

"Those protesters are for you?" Barnwell said with a laugh. "Now you know you've made it."

Tommy grimaced. "I was just trying to earn some money endorsing a product. So what if I hunt deer? I happen to like venison, and if there's extra meat I always donate it to a food kitchen."

"Now you're under a microscope. You've become a star," Barnwell said.

Tommy was perplexed.

"You'll get used to it," Barnwell said. "With stardom comes criticism. It's all part of the ride."

When Tommy got outside, a media crush descended on him. There weren't just reporters from the Atlanta area but national media as well. *The New York Times*, *Los Angeles Times*, *Chicago Tribune*, and *Sporting News* were in attendance, along with Florida television stations and online outlets, including *Yahoo Sports*.

So, this is what it's like to be a star, he thought to himself.

"Has the World-Series performance sunk in yet?" a reporter fired off. "What are your goals for this season?"

"It's been a wild ride, for sure," Tommy said. "I'm just trying to stay focused on my pitching. Our goal is to win back-to-back World Serieses." He figured that was how to say the plural.

"What did you do in the off-season?"

"I just rested my arm and basically chilled."

"You didn't do any throwing?"

"No."

"We saw you in plenty of ads," one guy chimed in.

"Everyone's gotta make a living," Tommy quipped.

"Your new contract pays you $42 million over two years. Do you feel pressure to live up to that?"

Tommy hesitated before answering that question. "I don't want to think about that. I'm just going to go out and win ball games."

"No worry about a sophomore jinx?" someone asked. "It's going to be tough to top your rookie season."

"Yeah . . . er, I'm looking to accomplish even more, probably win twenty games," Tommy said, staring off into space.

"How did you feel about seeing protesters outside the ballpark?"

"I have no comment on that."

"Tommy, what do you think about the drop in major-league attendance last year. Is baseball dying?"

"I don't think so," he said. "For me, it's never been better."

After about fifteen minutes, Tommy broke off the interview session. "I gotta get loose, guys," he said.

But as he jogged to the field, a couple of camera crews chased him down for exclusive interviews. "I really have to warm up," Tommy said, looking out at his fellow pitchers before grudgingly agreeing to the requests.

A year ago, no one cared about interviewing Tommy. He was the invisible man of Single-A baseball. Now he was a media star. People cared about his thoughts. Maybe too much.

"You ready to join us now," Barnwell said, "or do I need an appointment to see you too?"

Tommy smiled at Ty and waved his hand dismissively. "It's flattering, I have to admit. But I'm not sure if I'm ready for this," he confided. "Look what I got the other day."

He reached into the pocket of his baseball pants and pulled out a crumpled letter. "This is from some ten-year-old kid with leukemia. He says his dream is to meet me."

Barnwell glanced at the letter. "So, meet with him. Invite him to a game."

"I don't have time for that," Tommy replied.

Ty frowned at his teammate. "Make time," he said in disgust.

"I don't know what to say to a sick kid, Ty. If he's dying, what can I do? What am I, Babe Ruth? Am I supposed to point to the bleachers and hit a home run for him?"

Barnwell smirked. "I know you can't do that. That lucky single you got in the World Series is probably the only hit you'll have in your entire career. But you can meet with the little fella and lift his spirits. That's part of your responsibility as a professional athlete. I get requests from families all the time."

"I'm just awkward with things like that," Tommy said. "I don't know what to say to someone who might be dying."

"Just be positive. Be friendly to him. What's his name, anyway?" He grabbed the letter from Tommy. "Bobby Wilson," he read off, "and he's from right around Atlanta—in Jonesboro. Invite him to a game, man. If you want, I'll join you for the meeting. I know how to talk to kids."

"I do too," Tommy said, not wanting to appear too socially clumsy. "It's just sick people who I struggle with."

"You struggle? Think about his struggle. Just be positive, and don't criticize anybody like you did Soto last season."

"Hey, Javier and I are cool now. I regret what I said. That's ancient history."

"Good," Barnwell said, handing back the letter. "Let's get our asses out to practice now. I'm already a day behind."

CHAPTER 31

Position players soon rolled into camp and the exhibition games began. Many of the games, particularly the early ones, were devoted to evaluating young players and discarded veterans who were trying to make the team. The latter group was closely scrutinized to determine who was washed up and who had a chance to contribute as a bench player.

Before he took the mound, Tommy had to wait behind a batch of new pitchers who were invited to camp. Even though he'd never been invited to spring training with the Braves before, he was now considered a "veteran."

One day, Blasingame approached him while he shagged fly balls in batting practice.

"Tommy, time to get you throwing hard again. We're playing the college kids Wednesday in a friendly exhibition. I'm going to start you and let you go three innings."

"The college kids?" Tommy didn't know what his pitching coach was talking about.

"Yeah, once in a while we play a Georgia college team to build goodwill around the state. We got the University of Georgia scheduled this spring. It will be an easy tune-up where you can work on a few things."

Tommy nodded. It might be fun since he'd never played college ball.

"I don't want you to embarrass these kids too badly. They've never seen anything like your fastball," Blasingame said, slapping Tommy on the back. "Just don't overthrow. Be careful not to hurt your arm."

The game had all the markings of a fun, casual afternoon. It wasn't even on the exhibition-game level, more like a scrimmage against amateurs.

But as Tommy warmed up that day, anxiety began to creep in.

"When are you going to throw your Tommy Gun?" Bagley asked.

Tommy tried, but it wasn't there. Instead, his fastball came in straight—and not very fast. He told himself not to worry. He hadn't thrown hard in nearly four months. He needed to get his arm back in shape.

But when Georgia's diminutive leadoff batter drilled a home run over the center-field fence, the whole ballpark seemed in shock. Bagley looked as surprised as Tommy. "What, did someone tell you this was batting practice?" he called out to the mound.

The Bulldogs mobbed their leadoff man when he got back to the dugout, like he'd just hit a homer in the bottom of the ninth to win the College World Series.

Tommy's fastball lacked pop, so he started to rely on his curveball and changeup. Mixing it up, he managed to get some outs, but the fastball was hit hard nearly every time he released it.

"You're too easy on these college kids," Showalter said with a smile as Tommy strode into the dugout in the first inning, trailing 2–0. "You trying to boost their egos?"

Tommy tried to laugh it off. "I don't want to show them too much," he said before slipping off to the end of the bench.

When Tommy's three innings were over, Georgia held an improbable 4–3 lead. He overheard one Bulldog remark to a teammate, "I didn't see him throw that Tommy-Gun pitch once."

Patrick Walker and others couldn't resist needling. "I bet those kids can't wait to get back to their dorm and brag that they got a hit off the Browning Rifle, the World-Series hero," the reliever said mockingly. "Now they think they'll be pros."

"Nice job, man. You just made Georgia the SEC favorite," Barnwell cracked. "You've got my guys at Vandy shaking."

Tommy tried his best to laugh it off. After all, the outing meant absolutely nothing. But as he left the dugout following a 7–6 Braves win, he kicked the Gatorade cooler, nearly knocking it over.

CHAPTER 32

Under a cloak of darkness at midnight on March 26, Newnan and other areas in Coweta County, Georgia, were hit by a devastating tornado packing 170-mile-per-hour winds. The tornado traveled thirty-nine miles in fifty-three minutes and was a mile wide.

The powerful winds ripped away the roofs of homes over a hundred years old, and trees from their roots. West Newnan was hit particularly hard, but the historic and quaint downtown was largely spared. Newnan High School was severely damaged.

The fury and abruptness of the tornado momentarily paralyzed the city of forty-five thousand situated forty miles southwest of Atlanta.

When Tommy learned of the tornado, he called his parents later that morning. They told him they were safe; the family house was slightly damaged but still standing. Still uneasy, he asked Showalter for permission to leave training camp and drive up to his hometown to see his family. He also wanted to check on his new home under construction.

"Sure, Tommy. Take two days," the manager said.

Seeing the destruction in person was eye-opening. Seventy houses were completely destroyed, and 120 suffered major damage. More than twelve thousand local residents were without power. Two of those residents were his parents.

Tommy pulled up the driveway to see debris strewn all over the property of his childhood home. He was clearing tree limbs and blown-off shingles in the yard when his mother opened the front door and stepped outside.

"I guess it took a tornado to hear from you again," Evelyn said.

Molly, the family beagle, bolted past her and made a beeline toward Tommy.

"Hey, Molly. How are you, girl?" Tommy petted the dog as she ran circles around him, wagging her tail frantically like windshield wipers set on high speed. Her throaty bark still sounded too deep for a little dog.

"We've got some cleanup to do, but we'll get it done," Evelyn called out from the front steps.

"Just lending a hand, Mom. Where's Dad?"

"He went out to check on the neighbors. We're all without power."

"You don't have a backup generator?" Tommy asked.

"Never bought one," Evelyn said. "Didn't see this coming. Come on in and have something to eat. We have to use up what's left in the fridge before it goes bad. Maybe we can buy some ice and keep the meat in a cooler."

Tommy went inside to visit, embracing her at the doorway. His parents lived in a modest ranch house, and it was chilly inside, but the place offered the warmth of childhood memories.

"Mom, do you want me to get you and Dad a hotel until the electricity is back?" he asked.

"Not right now, Tommy. We'll see how long it's out."

"You know, I can buy you and Dad a new house if you want. Would you like that?"

"That's sweet of you, dear, but we like it here. I'd hate to leave our neighbors."

She searched her kitchen closet and frowned. "I don't know what I can fix you without being able to cook. I'd make you a sandwich, but I don't know if the cold cuts are still good. They've been around about a week. How about a bowl of cereal? I think the milk's okay."

"Nah, I don't need anything, Mom." Tommy motioned for her to sit down at the kitchen table with him.

"How's your phone? Is it still charged?" he asked.

"Only 20 percent."

"Let me take it and I'll find someplace to get it charged. Maybe I can do it from my car."

"When the power comes back on, how do we get our cable back? I'm missing my series on Netflix."

"It will still be there," Tommy said. "You just reboot the system. You know how to do that, or Dad does. The cable company will walk you through it. Anything else on your mind?"

"I saw a snake the other day in our yard," his mom blurted out. "It was really long and black. It scared me."

"Black, huh," Tommy said, trying to picture the reptile. "It could have been a cottonmouth, but they usually live near water. It's probably a black racer. They're harmless. In fact, they're good. They eat mice and insects."

"Yeah, well I hope I never see it again."

Tommy bent down to pet the dog. "Molly's looking good. A little white around the muzzle, though."

"Well, she's getting on in years. She must be at least twelve. I'm not sure she'll do any deer hunting with you anymore."

"Mom, for a hound, Molly never was much of a hunter. She won't even chase rabbits. When I take her out, all she wants to do is roll in the grass."

Tommy wanted to check out his old bedroom. As he made his way down the hallway, he spotted a large insect and stepped on it.

"Oh, those Palmetto bugs always seem to get into the house," Evelyn said, more than a little disgusted.

Tommy chuckled. He considered them to be cockroaches. "Palmetto bug" was just a nice Southern name for them.

The old bedroom was transformed into a guest bedroom. His trophies and posters were packed away, wiping out vestiges of his youth. At the sight, his heart sank. The only memory still standing was a prom picture of Tommy and his high-school sweetheart.

"Have you stayed in touch with Jennifer at all?" Evelyn asked.

"No, I haven't seen her since high school. She went off to college and I was busy with baseball," he said.

He picked up the picture and examined it closely. The memory seemed so distant now. His hair was in a mullet back then—like his pitching hero, Randy Johnson—and he wore a thin mustache that looked like it sprang from a starter kit.

Tommy examined the house some more, but soon cut the visit short, satisfied that his parents were okay for the time being.

"Don't you want to stay and see your father?" Evelyn said. "I'm sure the neighbors would love to see you too. They were so thrilled for you in the World Series. We had everyone in our living room watching the games."

"I'll be back. I just have to check on my house," he said. "Give me your phone and I'll get it charged. I'll be back in a little while with food and ice."

Tommy swallowed hard and drove out to see his mansion-to-be on the outskirts of town. He nervously followed the last bend in the road, said a quick prayer, and caught a glimpse of the lot beyond some tall pines.

The house was still standing. The tornado had missed it.

Construction equipment remained undisturbed on the property. He walked through the house with a smile on his face, impressed with the progress the contractors were making. The house was not only spared, it looked gorgeous. He knelt to give God thanks.

Guilt crept in. *Why was my house spared—and our family house? What have I done to deserve such great fortune in life, while others suffer tragedies?*

Tommy drove around the city to survey the wreckage. Funny, he'd always viewed nature as something beautiful, but now he contemplated the random cruelty it could summon.

He was curious to visit Newnan High on LaGrange Street, where there was major destruction: broken windows and doors, extensive roof and structure damage. The athletic fields, where he enjoyed some of his happiest childhood times, were ravaged.

He knew he needed to help. That day he decided to open his checkbook.

CHAPTER 33

When he arrived back at spring training, Tommy was soon ushered back onto the mound. The regular season was less than two weeks away. He needed more innings.

That became abundantly clear when he faced the Twins, who touched him up for four runs and six hits over five innings.

He pitched even worse against the Red Sox, allowing two home runs in the first inning.

Those bad outings confounded both Blasingame and Showalter. They met to discuss Browning's problems.

"Maybe it's a mental thing," Showalter suggested. "You know, with the protesters hounding him at camp and the tornado hitting his hometown. Maybe they've been weighing on his mind."

"I think it has to be physical," Blasingame said. "But he hasn't said he's hurt."

"Could he have a dead arm?" the manager asked.

Blasingame shook his head. "It may look dead at times, but I don't see how that could be the problem. Tommy didn't pitch winter ball. In fact, I don't think he picked up a baseball all winter unless he was autographing it."

"Well, there you go. Maybe his mind's not on baseball. He's got too many outside interests now that he's a star."

"I don't know, Whitey. He seems pretty focused. Somehow he's lost his fastball, that crazy pitch he throws. We had him clocked at eighty-four miles per hour on the radar gun against the Red Sox."

"Is he gripping it different? Is his arm angle the same?"

"I've asked him about that. He's funny about it, Whitey. He won't ever show anyone his grip, like he's protecting a government secret or something."

Showalter's mouth dropped at that revelation. "Well, he must be throwing it different. There's none of that screwy movement and it's not exploding anymore."

"Let's see if he comes out of it," Blasingame said. "Could be he's just holding back for the regular season."

"I hope so," Showalter said. "Maybe he does have to pace himself. He's never gone through the grind of 162 games."

"Yeah, and we open in six days. We're better off holding him now for the regular season," Blasingame said. "He's scheduled to pitch Game 2 against the Phillies."

Showalter shook his head as he considered the big picture. "I'm counting on Browning to have a big year. That's why we didn't sign any free agents. I hope we don't end up regretting that."

CHAPTER 34

Under the promise of a sparkling spring day, baseball's regular season launched with celebration. The Braves were presented their World Series rings in a pregame ceremony before facing the Phillies. When his name was called, Tommy drew a standing ovation from the sellout crowd at Truist Park.

Two of those standing were Bobby and Gloria Wilson. Tommy met Bobby, a freckle-faced kid with red hair, and his mom, Gloria, before the ceremony.

"Thanks so much for inviting us to Opening Day," Gloria said with an arm draped around her ten-year-old son. "Bobby is absolutely over the moon, aren't you, Bobby?"

Bobby smiled shyly as he lifted his head back and gazed up at his hero.

Tommy squatted down to his level. "I'm sorry you're struggling with your health," he said in a hushed tone.

"I just feel tired a lot, Mr. Browning," said the youngster.

"Please, call me Tommy. I feel for you. It must be awful."

Gloria shot Tommy a disturbed look.

"I can't imagine being a kid and not being able to run around all the time," Tommy said. "That's just horrible."

Gloria cleared her throat. She jumped in before Tommy could say any more. "It's not all gloom and doom, Tommy. They've made great strides in treating children's leukemia. Ninety percent of children diagnosed with leukemia can be cured, thanks to advances in science."

"Really? I didn't know that," Tommy said.

Gloria hugged her son again. "Bobby is undergoing chemo, and he's getting blood transfusions with red blood cells. We know he's going to get better."

"Oh, uh . . . I didn't mean to . . ."

"I know you didn't," Gloria said, cracking a smile to put Tommy at ease. She tried to change the subject. "I wish my husband, David, could be here, but he's at work. We've got to keep those health-care benefits."

"How would you like to go down to the cage for batting practice?" Tommy said, putting his hand on Bobby's shoulder. "You can see major-league hitters up close."

"Wow, can we?"

Bobby was in awe as he watched his heroes on the Braves rocket baseballs into the stands. The balls practically jumped off their bats.

"Are you going to take batting practice?" he asked Tommy.

"I may slip in for a few swings, but Ty will be in the cage before me. He's pitching today."

"I wish you were pitching today instead of Ty. I'd love to see you on the mound."

Tommy didn't hesitate. "If you want, why don't you come back tomorrow when I pitch? Maybe your dad can come too. I'll get you more tickets, some box seats."

Tommy's eyes sparkled. "That would be awesome!"

"I see you brought your glove," Tommy remarked, pointing to Bobby's small Rawlings model. "Do you want to play catch?"

Bobby's face lit up like it was Christmas.

The two began lightly tossing a ball around. Tommy set up just five yards from his throwing partner and started slow to gauge how well Bobby could catch. He also wanted to make sure that Bobby didn't overexert himself.

Bobby seemed to have a burst of energy instead.

"Are you going to throw the Tommy-Gun pitch tomorrow?" he asked.

"I may," Tommy said, carefully sidestepping a promise. "I'm going to try, Bobby. I'm certainly going to try."

Just one day after the fans showered applause down on their conquering hero during the pregame ring ceremony, the ovation was reduced to a smattering of applause when Tommy exited the game in the fifth inning with Philadelphia leading 6–1.

He threw his glove into the dugout after being lifted following a mammoth two-run homer and took a seat alone in the corner of the dugout.

Barnwell, who was charting pitches, gave his teammate a few minutes to stew before going over to him. "Hey, man. It's a long season. Shake it off."

"I just don't have it anymore, Ty," Tommy said. "I lost my fastball. My arm's not the same."

"Yeah, the ball's not playing tricks anymore. We all see that," Barnwell acknowledged. "Just keep grinding. You'll get it back, dog."

Tommy was ill at ease. "I don't know if I will," he said.

Barnwell looked away in thought. "Maybe you've got a Samson thing going," he said. "You know, ever since you cut your hair you lost your pitching strength. A coincidence? Maybe not."

Tommy's dour expression never changed.

"I'm playing with you, man," Ty said. He patted Tommy on the shoulder. "You want a bottle of Gatorade?" he asked.

Tommy shook his head and Ty left him alone.

Subsequent starts weren't any better. By the end of May, the Braves' World-Series ace was saddled with an 0–5 record and an eye-popping 7.50 earned run average.

Again, there were whispers in the clubhouse. Was Tommy Browning just a fraud? Maybe he *was* using a foreign substance in the championship run. Why couldn't he make the ball do tricks anymore?

The *Atlanta Journal-Constitution* ran a story under the bold headline: "Gun Control." The subheading read in italics: "Tommy Gun suddenly no longer in Browning's arsenal."

The story caused a stir because it quoted unnamed teammates making disparaging remarks about Tommy. One said, "No one could believe what he did last year, and no one can believe how bad he's pitching now. Jumping from Single-A to World-Series MVP seems like a fairytale."

Tommy immediately suspected Patrick Walker as the source. To him, the strident tone of the quote sounded like something Walker would say.

Another anonymous quote read, "Seems like the fastball he threw last year was just a mirage."

But one source was more positive. "He's struggling, for sure, but I'm not giving up on Tommy. We owe him that since he won the World Series for us."

Showalter and Blasingame were more confused than anyone, excluding Tommy.

"I think we should send him to the bullpen, let him work on some things," Blasingame suggested.

"We can't have him closing games," Showalter said sternly.

"No, no, nothing like that. I can just keep an eye on how he's throwing and work him in for middle relief if the game isn't close."

The manager considered his options. "First, let's have him

examined by a couple of outside doctors. I know our team doc says Tommy's healthy, but maybe they'll find a small tear or inflammation that we don't know about."

"He's just got to get that fastball back," Blasingame said. "The changeup I taught him is a great pitch, but it's not worth a hoot if hitters don't respect your fastball. And they don't right now. He's clocking in at eighty-four or eighty-five when he used to throw high nineties. If there's not much difference between the speed of your fastball and the speed of your changeup, you've got problems."

"Yeah, I know." Showalter shook his head. "No one stays in the big leagues with a fastball in the mid-eighties these days. Tommy's fastball was unique. Now it's just plain inadequate."

CHAPTER 35

In early June, the Coweta County Fairgrounds hosted the Tornado Relief Concert. The charity event drew thousands on a beautiful evening.

Georgia Country performed a long set, highlighting musical hits by local legend Alan Jackson. After opening with "Chattahoochee," they were greeted with warm applause.

"Everybody having fun?" lead singer Dale Howser yelled into his microphone. "Thank y'all for coming out tonight. We take care of our own down this way. My thanks to all the other musicians for being a part of this."

Howser slung his guitar around and looked appreciatively at the musicians on stage before turning back around and reading off a teleprompter situated in front of him.

"In the first two days after the storm, approximately twelve hundred volunteers helped out, and we think we'll raise two million dollars for tornado relief with this concert. Give yourself a round of applause."

The crowd roared its approval.

"Yes, you deserve it," Howser called out, applauding the crowd himself. "Unfortunately, Newnan High School was heavily damaged and the tornado threatened to cancel the senior prom. That came on the heels of the COVID-19 pandemic closing school for a spell. Man, these kids haven't been able to catch a break."

Howser looked at his fellow musicians, who nodded as the crowd grew quieter, reflecting on the recent devastating events.

"But I'd like to bring out somebody who donated a million dollars in relief, helping to save the prom through vouchers for free tuxedo rentals, while more than two thousand prom dresses were donated by members of the community for the lovely ladies. The prom went on as planned, outside the grounds of the Newnan Centre. This man's generous donation will also help restore the athletic fields at Newnan High.

"He's a Newnan native, and the pitcher who was named last year's World-Series MVP for the Atlanta Braves. Give it up for Tommy Browning!"

Tommy emerged from backstage wearing a "Newnan Strong" T-shirt, a Braves baseball cap, blue jeans, and sneakers. He raised his arms to the crowd and received a warm ovation.

Howser slapped his guest on the back. "Y'all want Tommy to sing a song with me? I know you know this one." He played the opening chords to "Gone Country."

Howser sang the first few verses himself. Then he handed off the next verse to Tommy and backed away from the mic.

People in the audience covered their ears. They'd never heard such awful, off-key screeching come from a singer's mouth. It sounded like caterwauling. Some words out of Tommy's mouth were virtually unrecognizable. Worst of all, he chose to substitute for a lyric:

"Look at them booties," he sang.

Howser made a split-second decision. He jumped in with Tommy for the last verse to rescue the song, and then indelicately bumped Tommy away from the microphone.

Tommy waved triumphantly to the crowd after they finished the "duet," while Howser leaned in close and whispered in his ear. "You must've had some mic trouble."

Tommy didn't know what he was talking about.

"Tommy Browning, ladies and gentlemen," Howser said,

raising his free hand only slightly. The applause was muted this time.

He grabbed Tommy by the arm. "Tommy, the line in Alan's song is about looking at boots, not booties."

"I know, I changed it. I thought I'd give a shout-out to the girls."

Howser's jaw dropped. He nearly dropped his guitar too, as Tommy bounded backstage, more than satisfied with his own performance.

While Tommy was at the Tornado Relief Concert, manager Showalter, pitching coach Blasingame, and GM Bailey were huddled together at Truist Park to talk about his future with the Atlanta Braves.

"We got the tests back from the doctors. They were all negative. Browning's arm is sound," Showalter reported.

Blasingame looked astonished. "There must be *something* wrong," he said.

"Not that the doctors could find," Showalter said.

The three men sat in silence for nearly ten seconds before Bailey finally spoke up. "I think we need to send him back to the minors, down to Triple-A. Let him work on his pitching and see if he can contribute again."

The other two men didn't resist the idea. Blasingame added, "Maybe Tommy can get his confidence back in Gwinnett. Going to the bullpen didn't help any."

Showalter was dumbfounded. "I can't believe we're sending our biggest star back to the minors," he said, shaking his head. "I don't know what happened to him."

The three men sat in silence, mulling over their predicament. Finally, someone spoke up.

"I sure hope he can get it back or reinvent himself," Bailey muttered. "We just gave Browning a forty-two million dollar contract—and it's all guaranteed."

When Tommy returned to Atlanta the next day, Showalter called him into his office.

"Tommy, how was the concert? Did you have a good time?" he asked.

"It was awesome, Skip. I got to go onstage and sing with the band Georgia Country."

"No kidding. That must have been a thrill. It was for a great cause; that's why I gave you the night off."

Showalter suddenly had a serious look on his face. "Tommy, I've given this a lot of thought. I'm sending you down to Gwinnett."

Tommy's face drooped, even though he knew in his heart a demotion might be coming. His numbers were plain awful.

"This will give you a chance to get some innings in and work on a few things. All players hit speed bumps in their careers. That's not unusual. Yours really came out of the blue."

Tommy looked down at the ground. The news was disheartening; his downfall had come so quickly. But he tried not to give up hope. Maybe he could regain his trademark fastball. He just needed to figure out how.

"What we're missing from you now is the swings and misses," Showalter added. "The hitters are all making good contact." He shook his head and scowled. "Let's face it, son. We're living in the age of strikeouts and home runs. It's all or nothing in baseball these days."

Showalter rose from his desk, as if to usher his former star out. "Work hard and we'll see you back up here soon," he said, extending his hand. "We have confidence in you, Tommy. We know you'll get back up here."

The two men shook hands before Tommy exited the manager's office. He trudged toward his locker to start cleaning out his belongings. That's when he ran into Ty Barnwell.

"'Sup, Tommy? How was the concert?"

"Good, Ty. Hey, I'm being sent to Triple-A."

Barnwell didn't look totally surprised. "Oh, I'm sorry, man," he said. "But we'll see you back here. They can't keep the Browning Rifle down for long." He gave Tommy a fist bump. "Remember what I told you once? Getting to the major leagues is the easy part. Staying here is the hard part."

Tommy reluctantly nodded.

"It's a business, dog, and they're invested in you. They're doing what's best for their investment."

"Yeah, I know," Tommy said before continuing toward his locker.

In a strange way, the demotion felt liberating to Tommy. He wasn't going to get knocked around on the mound in front of Atlanta fans anymore. Maybe he *could* rediscover his Tommy-Gun pitch in a quieter, more relaxed setting.

"Hey, Tommy," Barnwell said before Tommy had gone far. "You may have earned another place in history, besides your World-Series perfect game."

Tommy was interested but hoped it wasn't something to be ashamed of. "What?" he cautiously inquired.

"You know I'm the team's player rep, right? Management and the Players Association are about to agree on using the designated hitter in both AL and NL parks during the World Series. That means you could be the last pitcher to get a hit in a World-Series game."

Tommy gave Ty an appreciative smile. He was going to miss

Ty, he realized, as he walked out of the Braves clubhouse and into the unknown.

CHAPTER 36

Coolray Field, home of the AAA Gwinnett Stripers, was just thirty-five minutes from Truist Park, but to Tommy it might as well have been in the Pacific time zone. He and his career were tossed back in time.

Instead of facing the Dodgers, Mets, and Cardinals, he was now pitching against the Durham Bulls, the Norfolk Tides, and the Jacksonville Jumbo Shrimp.

As with most major-league ballplayers, a drop to the minor leagues brought with it a hard dose of humility. Back to bus rides and carrying your own bags. Say goodbye to charter flights, luxury hotels, and room service.

At least one player benefited from the move. In a weird case of karma, Hector Ramirez, the pitcher originally sent down to Gwinnett when Tommy was called up, rejoined the Atlanta Braves.

When Tommy joined the Stripers, he was treated like a celebrity. Players were thrilled to have a World-Series MVP on their roster. They all peppered him with questions about life in The Show.

"I would give anything just for a cup of coffee up there," one young pitcher said to him.

"A cup of coffee won't satisfy you," Tommy said. "You'll want the whole pot."

In his pitching debut, Tommy found that the talent level in Triple-A was better than he expected. While the hitters weren't as polished as those in the big leagues, they were miles ahead of his former Single-A teammates. Triple-A batters had weaknesses you could exploit, but it took some probing to find them, and more than a few were blessed with major-league talent.

He felt relaxed pitching in a cozy ten-thousand-seat stadium, but his Tommy Gun was still nowhere to be found against Norfolk. The one-time toast of Atlanta surrendered nine hits in a 7–5 loss.

One Tides player, who hit a home run, asked Tommy if he would pose for a selfie with him after the game. Tommy reluctantly agreed, like he was pleasing a fan.

However, in a few weeks the adulation turned to disrespect. Tommy was getting pounded night after night, and he was growing despondent. His fastball was still mediocre—even by Triple-A standards.

During a game against Jacksonville, an opposing player brazenly taunted Tommy after hitting a home run. "You've got nothing, man. You're washed up," he called out, as he stomped on home plate.

Tommy tried to laugh off the barb rather than cry. He was being told he was washed up by a Jumbo Shrimp.

But with a 1–5 record for the Stripers, a hefty ERA, and just three strikeouts per nine innings, Tommy's baseball future looked bleak. He tried to reinvent himself, even dabbling with a knuckleball, but nothing seemed to work. The Braves had doctors examine his arm again. Tests were still negative, revealing no injuries.

The Braves shopped their former star around, trying to work out a trade, but after scouting him there were no takers. His guaranteed contract for $42M was a major stumbling block.

In August, the Atlanta Braves announced they were swallowing the contract and releasing Tommy Browning outright. The media broke the news to the public.

"I'm going to get some tryouts," Tommy vowed. "I'm not giving up." However, he knew inside that his professional baseball career was over. He'd lost his fastball.

Desperation gripped him like it once had in Single-A. Then, out of the blue, he got a call from a little friend.

"Hi Tommy, this is Bobby," came the squeaky voice on the other end of the phone. "I want to thank you for sending me the autographed Braves hat. My dad says I should keep it in my room, but I wear it everywhere."

"Bobby Wilson, how are you? How're you feeling?" The sound of the child's voice buoyed his spirits.

"I'm doing great!" Bobby said. "The treatment I got worked. I'm feeling stronger."

"That's wonderful, pal. I'm so happy for you."

"Tommy, things will get better for you too. You'll see. I know it's tough not being with the Braves, but you'll be a star again. You'll beat this like I'm beating cancer."

"Thanks, Bobby." At that moment, Tommy's travails seemed trivial.

"The Tommy Gun will return. I know it will. Just stay positive."

"I will, Bobby. Hey, what are you doing with yourself these days?"

Bobby's voice rose with excitement. "I'm playing Little League," he said. "I'm a pitcher just like you."

When the phone call ended, Tommy thought back to the day he met Bobby. It started awkwardly, but he tried his best to boost the boy's spirits.

The irony wasn't lost on him.

It wasn't long before Tommy got a phone call from his agent.

"Tommy, this is Kevin," said the voice on the other end of the line. "Hey, I've got some bad news. Browning Arms Company is dropping you as its spokesman."

"What? Can they do that?"

"It's their prerogative," Shapiro said, "but they still have to fulfill the contract. They still have to pay you."

"How can Browning just drop me? I didn't sexually harass anyone. I didn't take PEDs or steroids." Tommy was completely disgusted.

"You committed a much bigger sin," Shapiro said. "You're no longer a star. And by the way," he added callously, "some people aren't convinced about that second one."

Tommy fired back at Shapiro. "What about my other endorsements? Are they dropping me too?"

"I haven't heard anything yet. But that may be coming. I'll keep you posted, buddy."

Tommy fell silent.

"It's been great representing you, Tommy," Shapiro said.

"Wait, are you dropping me too?"

"If that fastball ever comes back, you have my number," Shapiro said before hanging up.

Tommy's face grew red. He deleted Kevin Shapiro's number from his smartphone.

CHAPTER 37

Ed Sherman's sports column, titled "The Curious Case of Tommy Browning," appeared two days later in the *Journal-Constitution*:

"In the annals of Major League Baseball, inexplicable breakdowns have occurred in the careers of outstanding players. These breakdowns have baffled baseball followers to the point where they are still regarded as unfathomable.

"Pitchers Steve Blass and Rick Ankiel suddenly couldn't find the strike zone. Second baseman Steve Sax couldn't find first base. When all three left baseball they were remembered as much for their mysterious failures as for their lofty accomplishments.

"Consider Blass of the Pittsburgh Pirates, who is doomed to forever be accompanied by the words, 'Steve Blass disease.' Blass was one of the National League's best pitchers from 1968–1972, winning two games in the 1971 World-Series victory over the Baltimore Orioles. He remains the last NL pitcher to throw a complete game in Game 7 of a World Series.

"But after the 1972 season, Blass suffered a catastrophic loss of control. He just couldn't throw strikes. His ERA ballooned to 9.85 in 1973, and Blass was sent to the minor leagues. He never recovered and retired in 1975.

"Years later, Cardinals pitcher Ankiel, talented but not as accomplished as Blass, ran into similar woes. Ankiel, who once struck out major-league hitters at a rate of ten batters per nine innings, suddenly lost home plate too. So, what did he do? He reinvented himself as an outfielder. Ankiel played in the majors from 1999 to 2013, but that included six teams in a five-year span. One of those teams was the Braves.

"Sax's career nosedived as well. A five-time All-Star and 1982 NL Rookie of the Year, the Los Angeles Dodgers second baseman suddenly couldn't make a routine throw to first base. Sax committed thirty errors in 1983—mostly throwing errors. Fans sitting behind first base at Dodger Stadium started to wear helmets. No one was safe.

"Sax eventually bounced back. In 1989 he seemed completely cured, leading the league in fielding percentage and double plays. However, 'Steve Sax syndrome' did inflict other infielders after him.

"Tommy Browning's story is even more bizarre than those of Blass, Ankiel, and Sax. How do you explain a phenom who pitched the second perfect game in World Series history—and in doing so was named Series MVP—abruptly losing his stuff? Browning could still throw strikes, but suddenly he couldn't get anybody out. Unlike the other three, the problem seemed not to be mental but physical. Yet there were no reports of arm trouble. What caused Browning's famed Tommy-Gun pitch to lose fifteen miles per hour and its incredible movement, seemingly overnight?

"As pitchers age, they invariably lose speed on their fastballs and try to spot their pitches to survive. Many adopt the mantra of a real estate agent: location, location, location. But never have I heard of such a precipitous drop in velocity from a young pitcher without some injury to explain it.

"Some observers insist that Browning was once on performance-enhancing drugs. Yet he never failed a drug test. I don't believe Browning was on PEDs, but you never know. Strange things happen in baseball. Some consider Roger Clemens and Barry Bonds the best pitcher and position player, respectively, in baseball history. Yet they were both linked to steroids later in their careers. Why they would take them, I don't know. They were both headed to the Hall of Fame anyway.

"If performance-enhancing drugs fueled Tommy Browning's meteoric rise, he must have abruptly stopped using them.

"Others say Browning doctored the baseball, as evidenced by an ejection in a playoff game against the Milwaukee Brewers. However, in retrospect, that ejection seems unwarranted. He was never tossed from a game again.

"If you have the answer, please contact me or, better yet, the Braves. This is a confounding head-scratcher for the ages. I can't remember a baseball player whose career rose so spectacularly and then crashed so unexpectedly.

"There is one wacko in the United States Congress who suggests Browning may be an alien from outer space sent here to infiltrate American society. I won't even comment on that theory.

"But this much appears to be fact. At the tender age of twenty-three, The Browning Rifle is shelved for good. A baseball comeback seems extremely unlikely at this point. How can someone go from pitching a perfect game in the World Series to getting released the next season and no team signing him?

"This is one mystery that may never be solved."

CHAPTER 38

One year later, Celeste Freer rechecked her salary sheet and raised her eyebrows as she stared back at the job candidate sitting on the other side of her desk.

"We'd be extremely fortunate to have you as our baseball coach, Mr. Browning," said the Newnan High School principal. "I'm just surprised you're interested. It pays under $5,000."

"The money doesn't matter," Tommy quickly replied.

"Well, I'm sure you're comfortable financially after your professional career, but what makes you want to coach at this level?"

"I still love baseball," Tommy said. "The happiest days of my life have been spent on a baseball field. Those days are precious. That's why they play baseball on a diamond." Tommy cracked a natural smile and the principal emitted a giggle.

"Do you have any experience working with young adults? High schoolers?"

"I don't have much, really, except for some substitute teaching. But I think I'd enjoy working with teens, giving them the benefit of my experience as a player. I also have life experiences to share. I've seen the top and the bottom," Tommy pointed out.

Freer sat back in her chair. She was impressed with his candor. "I think it's wonderful you are willing to share those experiences," she said. "I'm sure you would be a valuable asset to the school."

Tommy straightened up in his chair. That was just what he wanted to hear.

"You have two other things going for you," she added. "You're an alum, which we always like, and you've already shown commitment through your generous donation. You helped save the prom and propped up the spirits of many students who were devastated by the tornado."

"I'm happy I could help. I loved my days at Newnan High, and I want others to enjoy them too."

"I have absolutely no doubt about your qualifications for the job," Freer said. "We do have a couple of other candidates to see, though. We're going to wrap up interviews this week. We'll be in touch."

Tommy surmised from the warm parting handshake that the coaching job might be his. He walked out into the school hallway, feeling confident.

It was around noon, and some teachers passed by, heading toward the teachers' lounge. He glanced up and was a few steps from an exit when one passerby caught his attention. He stopped, turned around to get another look, and called to her.

"Ellie Wainwright, is that you?"

The figure slowly turned around. "Well, well, if it ain't the great Tommy Browning. The last time I saw you, you were signing some girl's tits."

"I . . . uh . . . vaguely remember that," Tommy said, his eyes darting away.

Ellie looked at him suspiciously. "What are *you* doing here?"

"I interviewed for the baseball head coaching job."

"You slumming or something?" she said. "You're rich, even if you're out of baseball."

"I want to go back to my roots and try coaching," Tommy said. "Are you a teacher here?"

"I teach history," Ellie said emphatically.

Ironic, Tommy thought. He took a few steps toward her. "Ellie, I did miss seeing you after I got called up. Everything happened so fast."

"And ended fast, too," she said, her body language giving Tommy pause.

"You talking about my career?"

"No, I'm talking about us."

"I'm sorry. I felt like I got caught up in a whirlwind or something."

Ellie gave him an icy stare.

"Well, it's great to see you again. I hope we can get together now that I'm back home in Newnan, maybe have coffee or something."

Ellie showed no sign of softening. "I wouldn't count on it," she said as she flipped her hair and continued on her way. But a few steps later, she stopped and turned around again. Tommy hadn't even moved.

"Oh, and by the way, I was at the Tornado Relief Concert," Ellie said. "Stick with baseball, Tommy. You can't sing a lick."

CHAPTER 39

Just two weeks later, Tommy arrived at the teachers' lounge before noon and staked out a seat. A few teachers walked in and gave him suspicious looks.

"I'm the new baseball coach," he explained. They just nodded and got out their lunches from the refrigerator.

Finally, about ten minutes later, Ellie walked in. She didn't even notice Tommy as she grabbed her Cobb salad from the fridge and sat down at a table with two colleagues. Tommy waited until she was in her seat before strolling over from the far corner of the room.

"Hi, Miss Wainwright," he said in a pleasant voice.

"What are you doing here? Are you stalking me?"

The other teachers looked up from their food.

"I got the baseball coaching job," Tommy said. "I thought I'd drop by and tell you."

"Congratulations," Ellie replied coldly. She quickly returned her attention to the salad.

"Hey, Ellie, it's a beautiful fall day. Why don't we go outside? You can eat your lunch at a picnic table in the courtyard."

Ellie glanced at her watch. "I'm in a hurry. I've got class in thirty minutes."

"You've got time," Tommy said. "Come on, it's really nice outside. Let's get some fresh air."

"I can't today."

"Please. I came down here to see you."

Ellie hesitated. "I'm not sure I want to see you," she said.

"Oh, c'mon, let's just talk." Tommy leaned in to her. "Pretty please. I want to patch things up between us."

Still no response.

"What if I buy you season tickets to the Braves . . . or would you rather have them to the Peaches?"

Ellie finally surrendered a brief smile, a possible crack in her armor. She began to put her salad back in its plastic bag. "Okay, we'll try it," she said reluctantly.

Tommy eagerly moved toward the door. When Ellie got up from her chair, the teacher across from her pulled her over.

"Isn't that the guy who used to be a star for the Braves?" she whispered. Ellie nodded and the teacher's face homed in on Tommy. She gave Ellie an approving look.

Once outside they quickly located a table. The warm sunshine of a seventy-five-degree day seemed to lighten Ellie's disposition.

"You must think I'm crazy or something," Tommy said.

"I don't know," Ellie said. "There's always been a lot about you that can't be explained."

They both chuckled over that. "My intentions are pure," Tommy said. "I just want to be friends again."

"We were more than friends once," Ellie said, taking a bite of chicken.

"Maybe we can be again," Tommy replied, staring into her eyes.

"Did you ever think of making a baseball comeback? You're barely in your mid-twenties Don't you miss the fame?"

Tommy shook his head. "Fame isn't all it's cracked up to be, Ellie. And it's fleeting. The only comeback I want now is coming back to Newnan High School."

"Some people would call that downward mobility," Ellie said.

"I prefer to call it going back to my roots. What about you? How do you like teaching?"

"I love it," she said without hesitation. "And I'm thinking about going for the softball coaching position that's opened up."

"Cool! I hope you get it, Ellie."

Ellie glanced at the time on her phone. "I gotta go," she said before packing up her garbage and tossing it in the trash barrel. She saved the plastic iced-tea bottle for a recycle bin. "I've got five minutes to get to class."

They headed back to a side entrance to the school. "Can I see you again?" Tommy asked as he opened the door for Ellie.

"Oh, I'm sure we'll run into each other," she said, offering a slight smile. "The school's not that big."

CHAPTER 40

In April, Tommy sat in the dugout, thumbing through the latest sports news on his phone before his Newnan High players arrived for baseball practice. He came across a small headline: "Braves promote George Beavers from AAA."

A smile flooded his face. "Welcome to The Show, Bucky," he whispered to himself.

It was just two short years ago that Tommy had ridden the bush-league buses with Bucky, sharing their hopes, dreams, frustrations, and insecurities. Now his former catcher was getting a shot at stardom too.

Tommy's first season coaching high-school baseball was a triumph as well. The Cougars stood 25–8 and were headed to the state playoffs.

"Coach Browning, can I pitch batting practice today?" asked Manny Diaz, the first player to arrive at practice.

Tommy hesitated upon hearing the request. "Hold on a minute, Manny. Just get loose."

Tommy had an idea. He just wanted to bounce it off his assistant coach, Terry Griffith.

"Terry, I think we should reward Manny. The kid never gets into a game, but he volunteers to throw batting practice for us every single day."

"What do you have in mind, Coach?"

"Tomorrow's a non-region game and our last of the regular season. I wouldn't mind saving our pitchers for the playoffs.

What would you say if I said I wanted to reward Manny and let him start tomorrow's game?"

"Against Marietta? That could get ugly," Griffith said, sounding alarmed. "Manny's just a sophomore and he hasn't played a minute of varsity ball."

"I know, I know," Tommy acknowledged, "but I think he'd be thrilled. Don't worry, if he's getting lit up I'll pull him real quick, maybe move him into the field. I won't let the kid get embarrassed."

"That could happen," Griffith said. "Marietta's got a real good ball club. You know they have a guy with a full ride to Georgia Tech—if he doesn't turn pro. His name is George Washington, if you can believe it."

"His mama and daddy have a good sense of humor, naming him George," Tommy said, picking up his glove. "I hope he's class president."

Griffith returned the cornball humor. "I don't know about that, but I hear he commands the batter's box."

The two coaches laughed heartily at their own jokes. "Seriously, that Washington fella stands 6–4 and weighs about 230 pounds, from what they tell me," Griffith said. "Little Manny can't be more than 150 pounds soaking wet. I hope Washington doesn't hit a line drive back at the pitcher. It could knock Manny clear off the mound."

Tommy strolled over to Manny, who was loose and ready to go. "Manny, I'm going to pitch batting practice today. I want you to work with Coach Griffith and throw to a catcher, but for no longer than ten or fifteen minutes."

Manny looked disappointed but followed his coach's instructions.

When the players learned that Tommy was throwing BP,

they all pleaded for him to throw the Tommy-Gun pitch. "No, I don't do that anymore," he reminded them.

As the two-hour practice drew to a close, Tommy told Manny he'd be the starting pitcher the next day against Marietta High.

"I don't believe it. Thank you, Coach!" Manny said, grabbing Tommy's hand in appreciation. "I can't wait. I'm going to tell my papa to come. He's never seen me pitch."

"Not even in Little League?" Tommy wondered.

"No. My dad served in the Army in Afghanistan when I was little. I didn't have him around for a long time. But now he's back with us. He's got a good job with Coca-Cola.

"I can't believe I'm pitching tomorrow," Manny continued, his voice lifting. "I hope I can sleep tonight."

CHAPTER 41

The next day, Terry Griffith scanned the crowd while Tommy filled out the lineup card for the game against Marietta High School.

"Hey, isn't that Miss Wainwright in the stands?" he said, poking Tommy. "I don't recall ever seeing her at our games before."

Tommy's eyes shot up from his work. "That's Ellie, all right," he said, breaking into a sly smile. "We're seeing each other again."

"I didn't know you two were once a couple."

"For a brief time, but I acted like a jerk," Tommy said, kicking the dirt. "Funny, you know how in baseball they say hitting is about timing? I guess it's that way with relationships too."

He looked back at Griffith and sounded upbeat again. "It took a lot of work, but I finally won her back. We're going to the Ritz-Carlton at Lake Oconee next weekend. It's a promise I made a long time ago."

The Marietta team had arrived in Newnan and was taking infield practice. It was nearly game time.

"I'm going to have Jason DH for the pitcher," Tommy told his assistant. "That way Manny can concentrate on his pitching." He looked up from his scorebook. "By the way, does Manny have a curveball?"

"He's got a little wrinkle," Griffith replied.

"The old American-Legion roundhouse?"

"Something like that," Griffith said.

"How'd he look yesterday?" Tommy began to hope he wasn't making a big mistake.

"He looked okay," Griffith replied in a reserved tone of voice. "He throws strikes. He might get us through some innings."

Just then Manny rushed up to the coaches. "I'm going to warm up now," he announced. "I can't wait to take the mound."

"Just have fun, Manny," Tommy called out, as his first-time starter scurried off to find a catcher.

Griffith pointed to Marietta's first-baseman. "Hey, that must be George Washington. I wonder if he strikes a pose when he crosses the Delaware?"

Tommy playfully nudged his sidekick. "Why is he going to Georgia Tech? I bet George Washington University wanted him bad."

"All done, Coach," the Marietta coach said after throwing a high pop for his catcher. A couple of earlier attempts to hit a pop-up with the Fungo bat failed miserably.

Tommy waved back and brought out Newnan for infield. Before long, Manny joined them on the mound with a huge smile on his face.

Manny's second pitch of the game hit Marietta's leadoff batter.

"Shake it off, Manny," Tommy yelled from the dugout. "Infield, look for two."

The next batter poked a seeing-eye single between first base and second, before the third hitter lined a single to left. Bases loaded with Washington coming to bat.

"I was afraid of this," Griffith said. "Want me to get someone up to throw?"

Tommy hesitated. "Let me go out to talk to him," he finally said, calling time and walking slowly to the mound.

"Manny, buddy, how do you feel?" Tommy asked.

"I feel good. I'm going to get this guy," Manny said. He rubbed up the ball some more.

"Well, he's got a big strike zone," Tommy said. "Go get him, pal." He patted his pitcher on the back and returned to the dugout.

"Get Billy Chambers up," Tommy said to Griffith.

What happened next astounded everyone at the ballpark, but no one more than Tommy. Manny's first pitch to Washington left his hand like a floating knuckleball before picking up speed and exploding to home plate. Washington jumped out of the batter's box, and Newnan catcher Joey Manfredi batted the ball down with his glove in self-defense. Even the umpire jumped away before calling a late "strike." The pitch was clearly over the plate.

Dead silence gripped the ballpark.

Tommy racked his brain for an explanation. He hadn't taught anyone that pitch. He didn't know how to teach it. Was he seeing things?

Manny went into a windup and delivered again. Another mysterious pitch, another called strike. Manfredi almost caught this one. Washington seemed mesmerized and could only watch as the ball pounded into the pocket of the catcher's glove before tumbling out.

By now the fans were looking at each other, seeking confirmation for the bizarre sights before them.

"Tommy!" Ellie screamed out from the stands. She pointed at Tommy, and he responded with a shrug of the shoulders.

Washington looked in a daze as he trudged back to the Marietta bench after striking out. He pointed to his teammates on base. "I saw what they got to hit, and it wasn't what he threw me—no way," he said to the batter stepping out of the on-deck circle.

Manfredi took off his glove and wiggled his hand while grimacing in pain. He turned to the umpire and asked him to feel the hand. "Do you think it's broken?" he said.

Marietta left the bases full after Manny struck out the side. Tommy turned to Griffith. "We can't take him out now."

"We may have to," Griffith replied. "Joey might get killed back there."

Tommy was both delighted and befuddled to see his old pitch come from someone else's hand. Watching it from a dugout perspective made him truly appreciate the uniqueness of his Tommy Gun, how it fluttered before exploding. It also stirred up cherished memories of the World Series he helped the Braves win over the Yankees.

After six more innings of throwing the pitch almost exclusively, Manny Diaz finished with seventeen strikeouts, including three of George Washington, in Newnan's 3–0 victory.

Manny raised up his arms in celebration. Immediately, a man rushed out of the stands and onto the field to embrace him.

"Papa, I pitch good, right?"

"Manny, you were unbelievable. You didn't know you had it in you." The man lifted him off the ground in a bear hug.

Tommy marked the final K in the scorebook. He hurried out to congratulate his unlikely star and greet the man who he assumed was Manny's father. The man was clean shaven with close-cropped hair and wore dress slacks and a white button-down shirt.

"Mister Diaz, I'm so happy for Manny. He's just a great kid," Tommy said, extending his hand.

"Thank you, Coach," the man replied, smiling broadly. "Sometimes a simple act of kindness can have a bigger impact than you ever imagine. Sometimes all people need is some compassion and a chance."

"Well sir, I thought Manny deserved to start after helping us with batting practice all season," Tommy said.

"I'm talking about another act of kindness," the man replied.

Tommy looked puzzled. "I really don't know where Manny learned that pitch. I certainly didn't teach it to him."

Manny's father placed his hands gently on Tommy's shoulders. "You didn't have to," he said. "The Gift is still inside you. You just strayed from it for a while. But Coach, the Gift is meant to be passed on."

Tommy stared at him, bewildered.

"Nice to see you again," the man said, smiling. He gave Tommy a wink before turning and walking away.

Now Tommy was more confused than ever. "Have we met before?" he called out. But by that time, Manny's father was several steps toward the parking lot.

Then Tommy spotted a tattoo on the back of his neck. *Grace.*

"Ask, and it will be given you; search and you will find; knock and the door will be opened for you."

—*Matthew 7*

ABOUT THE AUTHOR

Bob Moseley is the author of two national award-winning sports novels, *Out of Bounds* and *Choker.* He has written for *Sports Illustrated*, the *New York Times,* and *Tennis Magazine* and is a career sports journalist.

Bob lives in Peachtree City, Georgia.

OTHER BOOKS BY BOB MOSELEY

Published by BQB Publishing

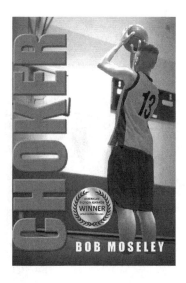

Sometimes you must dare to be different.

"*Choker* is a brilliant coming-of-age novel that immerses the reader in the drama of high school."

—Readers' Favorite Awards

Be careful what you wish for. Sixteen-year-old Mark Chamberlain always dreamed of playing in a state championship basketball game. But he never envisioned a nightmare performance that would bring utter humiliation and scar him as an outcast at school.

Classmates begin to call Mark "Wilt" Chamberlain because he melts under pressure. To top it off, Mark's father won't come to his games. When it feels as though the world is against him, with the support of a beautiful girl, Mark tries to summon the inner strength and courage to be different—just like legendary basketball star Wilt Chamberlain.

With another basketball season beckoning, Mark is given a precious chance for redemption.

"An engrossing sports story. The game descriptions really put the reader in the action and ring true."

—Literary Titan